Praise for *The End of Longing*

The End of Longing is a cleverly written piece of historical fiction…a complex story of mystery and intrigue…I was completely absorbed from the first page until the final scene.
BOOKSELLER AND PUBLISHER

Filled with allusions to nineteenth-century literature, history and mores, *The End of Longing* is distinguished by its sense of place, which is ironic really, as one of the themes in this richly layered book is that of travel and the peripatetic lives of the married couple at the centre of the story. But wherever his characters go, be it Japan, Canada or Honolulu, Ian Reid places us vividly there.
THE AGE

Reid scores a considerable success in recreating the hard-scrabble frontier towns of an age that is increasingly alien to our own…The reader encounters a pageant of nineteenth-century lives here…a realistic portrait of a bleak world.
AUSTRALIAN BOOK REVIEW

Ian Reid's fine and unusual historical novel…concerns a man who is a fugitive not only from the law and his past misdeeds but perhaps more essentially from his repressed better nature…Maybe – as Reid subtly suggests – it is the desire for revenge against the angels of his own nature that Hammond self-destructively seeks.
THE AUSTRALIAN

Compelling … intense … poetic … it stayed with me and has been hard to shake off.
SYDNEY MORNING HERALD

A tale rich in historical detail, creating two memorable and affecting main characters.

THE WEST AUSTRALIAN

Frances is a 30-year-old spinster living in Dunedin, New Zealand, restless and dissatisfied with the parameters of her life...Typical of colonial heroines, Frances is destined to satisfy a terrible curiosity – what is it like out there? Her husband, and perhaps her nemesis, is the Rev. William Hammond...Reid's exploration of William's background is suspensefully threaded through the book... very seductive.

WARRNAMBOOL STANDARD

An imaginative story of two people struggling to understand themselves and their relationship to the world around them.

WRITING WA

Skilfully realised...How well does any person know the 'truth' of another? This question underpins much of the novel and keeps the reader turning the pages...The gradual revelation of clues allows the reader to become the detective in pursuit of truth.

TRANSNATIONAL LITERATURE

Beautifully told.

LAUNCESTON EXAMINER

What Reid has done is to subvert the usual [family history] genre by telling the tale of an ancestor not at all respectable, and not at all predictable. It's based on documentation not at all reliable...Reid has invented good bits of his ancestor's story. Reid is also a poet, and he writes beautifully.

ANZ LIT-LOVERS BLOG

That
Untravelled
World

Ian Reid is a widely published author of literary and historical non-fiction whose writings have been translated into several languages. His poetry has earned him the Antipodes prize in the USA. His acclaimed first novel, *The End of Longing*, was published by UWAP in 2011. He lives in Perth where he is a Winthrop Professor at The University of Western Australia and Emeritus Professor at Curtin University.

That Untravelled World

Ian Reid

UWA PUBLISHING

First published in 2012 by
UWA Publishing
Crawley, Western Australia 6009
www.uwap.uwa.edu.au

UWAP is an imprint of UWA Publishing,
a division of The University of Western Australia.

THE UNIVERSITY OF
WESTERN AUSTRALIA
Achieve International Excellence

National Library of Australia
Cataloguing-in-Publication entry:

Reid, Ian
That untravelled world/Ian Reid.
ISBN: 9781742583969 (pbk.)
A823.4

Front cover image: Murray Street, Perth, looking east, 1920s, Ernest Lund
Mitchell, State Library of Western Australia BA1271/266

Back cover image: Applecross radio mast, 1935, Stuart Gore,
State Library of Western Australia 031846PD

Cover design: James Allison

Typeset in 11 pt Bembo by Lasertype
Printed by Griffin Press

This project has been assisted by the Australian Government
through the Australia Council, its arts funding and advisory body.

Australian Government

To Zoë and her kith

Yet all experience is an arch wherethrough
Gleams that untravelled world whose margin fades
Forever and forever when I move.

Tennyson, Ulysses

Part 1

1912 – 1915

One

She seemed to have left without any trace, and her parents too, as if whisked inexplicably into utter oblivion.

All his anxious questioning led nowhere. There wasn't a single person who could tell him where they might have gone, or why. The sheet of brown paper tacked to the bakery door said bluntly, in a thick pencil scrawl, CLOSED. No explanation.

At first he told himself that some urgent family matter must have summoned them suddenly – perhaps the illness or death of a relative somewhere away from Perth. No doubt they would soon return. In the meantime, Nellie would surely write to him, clearing it all up. Knowing how intense his feelings were towards her, she'd want to reassure him with some words of shy affection. But days went by with neither letter nor reappearance.

The neighbours said they had no idea at all. Even the Biddles, right next door, had heard and seen nothing. 'Not a squeak, not a glimpse,' Cec Biddle kept repeating; and to the notebook-wielding constable who seemed to expect a fuller statement he added with a final flourish, 'Not the slightest glimmer'. Old Mrs Polly Milligan, the jowly one across the street who took pride in knowing everybody's business, shook her head in a pantomime of puzzlement until her wattles jiggled. 'Just vanished into thin air,' she averred worriedly, clucking with a slack tongue against her palate.

Into thin air: it struck Harry as a strange notion. Hardly less fanciful to imagine some ghostly thickening of the ether had carried them off, a dense fog rolling slowly up the Swan River from Fremantle during the night like a silent vaporous wave to envelop the whole Weston family and spirit them away.

That all three of them had been somehow abducted was almost beyond belief; but that they could have departed of their own accord in secret, slinking off without so much as a word to him – or to anyone else, apparently – seemed just as absurd. Then, if not a forced removal or a furtive getaway, what had happened?

The Weston mystery was the talk of the village. Could be a money problem, Freddie Dingle said, could well be. Others nodded. George Weston didn't own the bakery, according to Polly Milligan – he'd been running it for years on a long-term lease from some fellow down Albany way, no-one knew who – and perhaps had got himself into debt and decided to skedaddle, being a church stalwart and not wanting to face up to the shame.

'But what if they're still in there?' wondered Marge Biddle as she bent down to fill a saucer of milk for the Westons' querulous cat. 'Murdered in their beds, might be?'

Tom Torrence, local cop, had waited several days before peering in through the Westons' windows and a further day before breaking one of them to get in and have a bit of a squiz. Half the street's residents gathered outside while he smashed the pane and clambered through, sweating, tearing his sleeve, muttering to himself.

'Any sign of foul play?' a voice called out eagerly as he emerged at last. He shook his head.

'Nup. Most things in their usual place, looks like, more or less, 'cept for clothes – nothing much left in the wardrobes or chest of drawers. Not sure about some other stuff. Hard to tell what mighta gone. Whether they coulda taken it away themselves, or robbery or what. Anyway, got a report to write up. So off ya go now, all of ya.'

For a week Harry kept a lid on his fears. Some kind of message would reach him before long. But nothing came. Expectation gave way to alarm, and then subsided into a dull ache.

Troubled nights made the mornings weary. He found it hard to stay asleep for more than an hour or two at a time. Waking with a start from dreams of confusion, he would stare into the inscrutable darkness, sit up in his narrow bed, rearrange sheet and pillow, lie down again, turn this way and that, while his mind went tick-tock-tick through every obscure and agitated possibility.

'I feel sort of numb,' Harry told Sven as they unloaded crates at the little jetty and stacked them on the cart. But not just drowsy, he thought, plodding along the sandy track beside the straining horses and their load. It was the shock, too – mixed up miserably with a sense of powerlessness, and with sheer perplexity.

It would be a long while before he could begin to free himself of this troubled tangle of feelings, and years more before he knew there are some secrets so painful to discover that they may need to be closed up again.

⤸

As the enigma of Nellie's sudden disappearance deepened, Harry sifted through every retrievable moment of the four months since he met her, trying to recall each conversation, looking for any shadowy hint that he could somehow have missed at the time. Although the wireless station project demanded close attention throughout the working day, part of his mind kept slipping back distractedly to those early weeks. He thought of the things that had brought them together.

Their first encounter had begun inauspiciously.

WESTON'S FAMILY BAKERY: the lettering on the front wall was matchstick-plain. Turning the loose brass knob and pushing the door open, Harry found the shop dim and unattended. A yeasty smell drifted warmly through it. When he tinkled the bell on the counter there was the sound of someone moving about in a back room. He saw on a shelf, as he waited, the framed text admonishing customers with the words *Man shall not live by bread alone*. He recognised it as a biblical injunction, but tried impulsively to turn it into a little joke when a young woman emerged – shapely, he noticed, and comely – wiping her hands on an apron and disconcerting him with a sunbeam smile of welcome.

'G'morning, miss. Just a half loaf please. And I assure you,' he added in a facetious tone, pointing to the stern text, 'I'll be having plenty of cheese with it.'

She cancelled her smile with a prim reproof. 'My father wouldn't like to hear you making fun of God's word.'

'Sorry,' he said, twitching his shoulders in a half-shrug of chagrin. He'd always been told he had a way with words, the gift of the gab, so it was galling that his usual fluency had deserted him at such a moment.

But she didn't seem to hold it against him. When he went back a couple of mornings later to buy another loaf for his lunch-bag, she greeted him with the same sparkle that had gladdened him the first time.

'Making more cheese sandwiches?' she asked. A dimple of amusement flickered near her pretty mouth. Her eyes were as bright as a candle flame.

'Whatever I put between the slices, your bread's perfect for it,' he declared, conscious that it sounded like a stilted advertisement. Taking the loaf she placed on the counter, he picked at its kissing crust, put a little piece in his mouth and chewed appreciatively. 'Mmm. Lovely!' he said, nodding like a clown. 'Straight from the oven, isn't it? Thought so. Mmm.' Prolong this transaction somehow, he told himself. Ask her a question, chatter about anything. But luckily she had her own string of queries.

'Put the sandwiches together yourself, do you?' she asked.

'Certainly do. Who else'd be doing it for me?'

'So you live alone?'

'Not exactly, miss. I lodge at a boarding house just along the road there, past the Mends Street corner.'

'With the Rivens?'

'Yes. You know them?'

'We see them on Sundays, mostly. They worship at the same chapel as we do.'

His turn now. Stalled in self-consciousness, Harry pursed his lips and whistled a scrap of a tune while trying to think

7

how to keep the conversation going. A small grizzled cat emerged, as if in response to the whistling, and approached him with cautious tread. Glad of the diversion, Harry knelt and tickled its ears. It favoured him with a slow wide yawn.

'Family pet?' he asked the young woman.

'Not exactly. Not in the pampered sense. She's supposed to be working for her keep – as a mouser. Doesn't do a bad job, actually, though she's getting on in years.'

'Seems friendly now, but I guess she'd frighten the daylights out of a rodent. Have you given her a name?'

'We just call her Beastly.'

Harry toyed for a moment with the idea of a forced joke about Beastly and the Beaut, but dismissed it. Better to draw her into an exchange of information: getting to know about her would probably be easier if he mentioned a few things about himself.

'I've been here in Western Australia just a couple of weeks,' he told her. 'Came over from Sydney. On a P&O mail steamer, RMS *India*. Arrived New Year's Day.'

'So Sydney's your home? Yes? Then why have you come to Perth?'

'Well, I'm a junior engineer, y'see, brought over here to work on…'

But before he could tell her anything about his job, let alone about all the plans, enthusiasms and stories that he had a sudden urge to share, a man's voice called out sharply from one of the back rooms: 'Nellie!'

She responded at once to the peremptory tone as if tugged by a string. 'Coming, Dad!'

'Name's Harry Hopewell,' he blurted as she turned away, and her acknowledging smile seemed to anticipate further exchanges. Nellie: he savoured her name as he left the shop. So it's Nellie.

When he tried afterwards to picture the details of her face he couldn't be quite sure of the colour of her eyes, or hair, or exactly what her nose looked like, but her shy smile stayed with him. And her voice, pleasantly modulated – he could hear again the hint of gaiety at the edge of her words.

In contrast, the sound of her father's gruff voice had led Harry to imagine an ogre, but when he encountered him a couple of days later on his next visit to the bakery the small thin man behind the counter didn't look formidable. His dour unsmiling manner was perhaps just a mask for diffidence. Nothing ventured, thought Harry, clearing his throat as he paid his money and picked up the warm loaf. 'Ah – Mr Weston…' he began, and then hesitated, feeling a flush in his cheek and sweat in his armpits. Weston did something quizzical with a tufty eyebrow.

'Your daughter, sir – Miss Nellie: I wonder whether you might let me take her to the zoo this Saturday afternoon. If she agrees, that is. I haven't asked her yet.'

There was a long pause. Weston brought his hands together slowly and cracked his knuckles; then, frowning, he adjusted his spectacles.

'You're Hopewell, I suppose?'

'I am, sir. Harold Hopewell.'

'Nellie mentioned you. Doesn't usually talk about our customers, so you must've sparked a bit of interest somehow. I don't doubt she'd like to go to the zoo in your company. But we know nothing about you. Whaddya do for a living, lad?'

'I work for Australasian Wireless. We're building the new station on the hill behind Applecross.' Harry squared his shoulders proudly.

'Heard something about it. Can't see the point, I must say. But I suppose it pays well. How old are you?'

'Twenty. Well, nearly twenty, to be precise.'

'I prefer precision. New to these parts, aren't you?'

'Yes. Just arrived from Sydney in early January. The company sent me here for the wireless station work. I'd been employed on the other station that the government commissioned, the one at Pennant Hills. Twin projects. There aren't many people who know about setting up the equipment, you see. Very specialised.'

'Hmm.' Weston wrinkled his brow, thrumming the counter with his fingers. 'Answer's no. You're still just a young fellow, and I won't let our Nellie go anywhere with you on your own. Tell you what, though: you can come along to the zoo with the three of us – Nellie and Mrs Weston and me. How's that?'

Harry grinned with relief.

'Oh, splendid, yes, certainly, thanks very much Mr Weston. Two o'clock be convenient? It'll take me till then to get back from the hill and clean myself up and walk here.'

'All right, lad. We'll expect you at two on Saturday.'

As he left the bakery and made his way to the jetty with bouncing stride and jaunty whistle, Harry felt energy surging in his veins. He swung his arms vigorously. If there had been no-one else around, he would have skipped like a child. Saturday, eh? Saturday!

He didn't much mind, really, that Nellie's parents would be coming with her as chaperones. It could even be quite pleasant, linked like that to a family group. Here in Perth he'd been feeling the absence of his own mother and father. First time away from home, and the boarding house was a poor substitute. Perhaps the Westons, as they got to know him, would regard Harry as almost… But whoa! He was getting ahead of himself. The weekend would arrive soon enough. He needed to iron his best shirt and perhaps buy a more respectable hat.

Meanwhile there was his daily stint at the busy site on the bare hill. He was learning to be patient: he would come into his own soon enough, when the pieces of big equipment arrived, and until then there were plenty of ways of making himself useful around the place. Measurements and calculations needed to be checked and rechecked against the drawings. He could give a helping hand with the barbed wire fencing and with some of the cartage and unloading of building supplies. And Bill Flynn, the fussy old electrician, wanted to discuss every little detail of the transmitter arrangements with him.

Harry was impressed by the rate of progress. The aerial components had come earlier, before his arrival in Perth. By the time he turned up on the job the Public Works team had already laid the foundations, supervised by Schank and Larrson. He knew from the Pennant Hills project that these two worked together in unison, like Siamese twins, but seeing them again side by side made him smile. They could hardly have looked more different: Max Schank, the mast engineer, was a ruddy-cheeked bullock of a man; Sven Larrson, the rigger, a tall skinny streak with a pale pocked face. Evidently they'd wasted no time at this Applecross site: the three concrete towers were in position to anchor the aerial, and further away the men had dug a ring of holes to take the smaller tethering blocks. Those restraints would be vital, he understood that. Some days the wind had startled him with its sudden ferocity, and a steel spar rising to 400 feet above the hilltop could hardly withstand such gusting unless it had several strongly fastened copper guy wires to secure it. Schank told him it would stand on large glass insulators and weigh 50 tons. Its base could take that burden comfortably: solid and enormous, with part of it buried deep below the surface. An amazing contraption, this mast, thought Harry. It would be the tallest structure in Western Australia. No man-made thing of comparable height for thousands of miles north, south, east or west. Nothing quite like it anywhere in the whole country except the prototype back in Sydney.

On his first day there, Harry had stood beside Schank in the shadow of one of the concrete towers, and looked out across the wide stretch of the Swan River. The weather was unusually still, and the glassy surface of the river gleamed beneath an unclouded sky. Schank pointed down to the water. 'Calm as a milkpond!' he exclaimed.

'Millpond,' said Harry.

'Eh?'

'Millpond, not milkpond.'

Max Schank crinkled his forehead at this obtuseness. 'It's just a saying,' he explained, as if instructing a child.

Harry let it go, turned and gestured towards the structures rising behind them. 'You've got a hell of a lot done here in a short time,' he said.

Schank grunted and nodded. 'Been verking like a Trojan horse,' he declared. Harry hid a smile. He liked to hear big Max's thick German accent and his frequently muddled phrases.

Both the main buildings were already completed apart from facings and fittings. Harry liked the look of them. One was the Engine House, where the huge diesel-driven generator and the transformer would sit; the other, the Operators' Building, would contain transmitter, receiver, and switchboard. Water tanks were in place behind them, and a windmill to drive the pump for a well. A space was marked out for a third building, to store fuel and other supplies. Meanwhile the Public Works blokes were going to start work soon on the cottages near the foot of the hill, so that the station manager and telegraphists could take up residence with their families.

To be part of such a marvellously innovative project, at the forefront of technical knowledge! Harry could hardly believe his luck. They were laying a foundation stone for the modern world.

The river journey that brought Harry to Applecross each working day and took him back again at the end of the afternoon was always invigorating. He liked to stand at the rail, thinking fondly of Nellie, feeling on his face the warm air that was sometimes damp with spray, and watching the wake recede. Often, as the paddle steamer left the South Perth jetty behind, gathering pace and moving out into the channel beyond Mill Point, Harry would see that it was under playful escort: a pair of undulatory dolphins just a few yards away rose and arched and dived and rose again, as if in happy mimicry of the boat's great wheel, their finny backs turning sleekly like serrated rotary discs. It seemed, at that stage, an omen of good fortune.

Two

On the southern side of the river, social life revolved around the big zoo. Harry knew this even before he arrived in Western Australia: one of his fellow passengers on the P&O steamer, a chatty young bank clerk returning home to Perth, told him all about it.

'It's not only to gawk at the menagerie that people go to the zoo,' said his informant. 'There's all sorts of entertainment too. Fashion parades. Mineral baths. Concerts in the evening. Plenty of sporting events – tennis tournaments, cricket matches, croquet. Pony rides for the little ones. And picnics, of course – they're popular even on the hottest days. There are shade houses and shelter sheds, you see, fringing the grass oval.'

Harry soon found that everyone in South Perth was ready with an opinion about the zoo's greatest attractions. The topic often came up over meals at the Rivens' boarding house. Mr Kenneth Riven worked at the zoo, supervising all the arrangements for looking after the animals, from their food supplies to the cleaning of their cages, and he had to 'keep the keepers on their toes', he said. Harry would listen intently as the half-dozen others around the dinner table plied Riven with questions and gratuitous advice.

It was a strange group of lodgers, and Harry characterised them colourfully in a letter to his parents, who had always found his flair for description amusing.

There's Mr Wilt, he wrote.

No-one knows his first name. Ancient. Thin as a pipe-cleaner. He shuns newspapers as if they're unclean and quotes biblical verses relentlessly. Then there's Dicky Billings, he's a clumsy butcher's apprentice, one finger gone already, with a lolling tongue that thickens his speech into a heavy lisp. Mrs Dottie Crump spends more time in our communal bathroom than the rest of us combined. She's an unmerry widow, indiscriminate with her powder-puff, who murmurs constantly but seldom audibly. Basil Marsh is a clerk with the Municipal Council Office. He's endowed with a raptor-like beak, yet he's as timid as a wren! And the Carters: they're twin brothers, a lumpish pair, often unemployed, who share a propensity for inebriation and a moody passion for fishing from their rowboat out on the river. To Mr Riven, we must seem like just another coop of curiously assorted creatures.

It amused Harry that his fellow residents agreed on nothing except their opinions about the zoo's inadequacies. Ostriches were all very well, but not different enough from emus to deserve much attention; zebras were nothing special either, little more than stripy horses; the tiger was impressive, yes, though hardly distinguishable in shape from a hulking tomcat. Why didn't the zoo have some really grotesque beasts, like a giraffe or a rhinoceros? By the way, couldn't Mr Riven do something about the pong from all that manure on the garden beds? Worse than the stinky monkey house. And so on. It was obvious that Riven enjoyed this tea-table chatter. He would smile in a self-satisfied way, stroke the red hair of his moustache, and puff on his little bent pipe.

Like every other February day in Perth, this Saturday was long, sweaty and glaringly bright under a cobalt sky stretched taut as a tympanum. Yet Nellie's presence made it unlike any other day for Harry.

He knew that the big paddle-steamer, both decks crammed full for each trip, had been ferrying its flocks of day-trippers from Barrack Street on the city side across to the Mends Street jetty. From there it was only a five-minute walk to the zoo entrance on Suburban Road. As Harry and the Westons approached the queue they could hear a hum of animated talk. Fidgety children, squeaking with anticipation, hopped from one foot to another. Fathers were pressing handkerchiefs to their brows and mothers toyed with little parasols.

'Gosh!' exclaimed Harry, squinting, shading his eyes with his forearm. 'I hadn't expected to find people waiting to get in at this time of the day. And look at the crowd inside – right along that avenue!'

'You haven't been here before?' Nellie asked. 'They say about a thousand visitors come through it on a Saturday – remarkable, really, when you think that the whole population of Perth is just over 100,000. I remember Mum and Dad brought me along to see the tiger when I was very small

– and I cried because I'd never seen so many people milling around. They scared me more than the tiger.'

Her soft giggle, Harry thought, must be one of the loveliest sounds any human voice had ever produced.

He paid a shilling to cover admission both for Nellie – he was careful to call her 'Miss Weston' – and for himself; her parents insisted on buying their own tickets.

'First time I've visited *any* zoo,' Harry announced. 'So I don't really know what I'm in for, apart from a collection of exotic beasts.' Intermittently there were strange sounds in the background, squeals and screeches and rumbles. He had no idea what kinds of creatures they came from. As he and the Westons made their way slowly along the curving paths, the sheer size of the place astonished him. He had imagined a compact cluster of cages, and knew there would be picnic spots, miscellaneous plants and various amusements. But it was far more spacious than he could have guessed, cleverly landscaped, and replete with ingenious attractions. Here were extensive areas of parkland, long sweeping tree-lined avenues, garden displays, ornate fountains, gazebos, rotundas and a large array of uncrowded animal enclosures.

It was all so engrossing that for much of the time he forgot to use his proud new possession, the Box Brownie camera he'd brought along with him. But he did take a couple of photographs of Nellie in front of the elephant enclosure. The grey giant moved so ponderously that there was little risk of a blurred image. Some of the other creatures just wouldn't keep still.

'Those baboons over there,' said Harry, pointing, 'the ones with red bottoms and pale faces – they look just like clowns, don't you think? And acrobats too, the way they cavort around, even with babies clinging to their necks. It's a family circus!'

It struck him that the zoo was full of families, both visitors and inmates: human families stopping to stare at captive families of monkeys, zebras, lions, turtles (or were they tortoises?), tigers, bears, fish and fowl, and dozens of other creatures, large and small. He thought of stories he had heard as a child.

'This whole scene reminds me of something my mother used to talk about,' he told the Westons. 'She'd come to Australia as a little girl, with her parents, and they were from the Shetland Islands, you see. Well, both of the old folks died before I was born, so I didn't ever hear their stories directly, but they must have gone over and over the cherished details of that strange little homeland of theirs on the far side of the world, and so my mum became the custodian of their memories. She'd often describe to me what she'd heard and half-recalled about the life they left behind. When I was very young I'd get her to repeat her Shetland tales. It sounded like a bleak, harsh place: stone, peat, the roar of angry seas, not much else. Everything stunted by biting winds and salt spray. Easy to understand why they'd left!'

An anxious thought made him pause momentarily. Was he talking too much? Would this seem to Nellie like tedious prattle?

But apparently she sensed his need for reassurance. 'Go on,' she said with an encouraging nod. They strolled on slowly.

'Well anyway,' he resumed, 'what popped into my mind just now was that each crofter's stone house was joined to the byre where they kept their cattle every night in summer and all day long in winter. And they'd have smaller animals right in there with them in what they called the but-end, where they all ate and sat and slept. People, cats, dogs, piglets, caddy lambs – all one family, like a little zoo under one roof. Think of the smell and noise! But my mother always spoke about it with affection.'

Nellie nodded understandingly. 'Growing up with animals would make anyone think differently about people, I suppose – how we relate to each other. Apart from our old mouser, Beastly, I haven't had any contact with cats or dogs or anything like that. My dad doesn't like the idea of pets, and we don't have any farming friends. So it's only here at the zoo that I get to see what different animals are like.'

'For my fourth birthday,' Harry told her, 'my parents gave me a couple of little creatures in a cage. An odd pair, a fat white rabbit and a little black guinea pig, but they'd snuggle up together like siblings. Their cage was near our back door, and I'd always go out and say goodnight to them before my bedtime. Well, one evening I got a big shock, and rushed inside sobbing and yelling, "My guinea pig has come to bits!" Dad ran out, and then I heard him burst out laughing. "Nothing to worry about, Harry," he said. "The guinea pig has had a litter of babies!"'

'That sounds like a story you've told a few times before, Mr Hopewell,' said Nellie. 'You tell it well. And your description of a Shetland crofter's house, too – very eloquent.'

'My parents gave me a love of words,' explained Harry. 'And storytelling was a big part of our family life.'

For Harry every moment of the afternoon was suffused with pleasure just because Nellie was at his side. Winsome, he thought. That's what she is. Perhaps not beautiful in the usual sense, but winsome.

They spent an hour or more sauntering from one exhibit to another. A few energetic animals caught their attention first. There was busy activity among the meerkats ('How would it feel to have a tail?' whispered Nellie) and in the tiny turreted castle for guinea pigs ('Like fancy rats in mottled cardigans,' said Harry). Chimpanzees put on a romping display. A pair of young goats kicked up their heels. But most of the animals were far from frolicsome. The bears seemed torpid if not morose, and Harry said so.

'Can't help feeling sorry for those creatures. Cooped in dirty concrete prison cells for us to gape at.'

Nellie's father shook his head, frowning. 'Don't waste your pity,' he said. 'Remember, the Lord gave us dominion over all dumb animals. They don't feel things the way we do. These bears have a good lazy life here. Free from harm. Food laid on for them every day. Somewhere to shelter from the weather.'

It was plain that on the rare occasions when Nellie's father spoke he expected others to defer to his views. Mrs Weston had a drooping manner and almost nothing to say; a nervous twitch of her lips seemed to be the nearest she could come to communicating. Her husband's habitual expression was a frown and he talked as if he had sand in his mouth. Untroubled by their lack of conversation, Harry chattered away to Nellie, whose shy and serious demeanour was softening by the minute. She had none of her father's Methodist dullness, and none of her mother's servility. A natural grace, he thought.

The heat seeped through their clothes and into their marrow. Hats and parasols were ineffectual. Harry could feel wet patches spreading under his armpits.

They came to a vantage point from where they could look down on a pair of lions sleeping in a patch of shade. Each time the male exhaled, a little quiver lifted part of his mane. Harry and Nellie stayed there staring at the pair while her parents walked on ahead. 'The colour of their hide – it's like honey!' she exclaimed, hands pressed together and fingertips against her mouth as if in worship. 'All the animals we've seen here are beautifully colourful, and all the people are wearing just white or black.'

'But I think you look…lovely in your white dress,' said Harry. *Maidenly* was the word he nearly used.

'Thank you,' she said with a demure smile. 'But white's very plain compared to that rich tawny tint that the lions' skin has – gorgeous, isn't it?'

Harry pointed his Brownie at the lions and squinted through the viewfinder. The male stirred, stood, sniffed at the lioness's tail then moved in behind her and straddled her rump. Before the pumping began, Harry quickly took Nellie's elbow, distracting her attention and steering her away from a scene that would, he presumed, make her blush. Or was it, perhaps, his own embarrassment that he was dodging? This flicker of carnality had smudged the afternoon's politeness.

He chattered nervously. 'You can see,' he said, turning their steps towards the vegetable beds, 'why it's called a zoological *garden*, can't you? Makes good practical sense, growing a lot of crops on site to produce food for the animals: all that lettuce, and what else, alfalfa isn't it? – and carrots, they look like, over there. Not sure whether those botanical displays' – he gestured towards the exotic tropical plants, the large fern grove – 'have some kind of scientific purpose, but anyhow they're magnificent, don't you think? I'd never have imagined there could be such lush growth in this hot dry climate.'

He felt vitality coiled within himself like a young frond ready to unfurl from one of those tree ferns.

'It's because of the artesian bore,' Nellie explained. 'Dad told me it was sunk when they constructed the site. For all the garden beds, and those fountains there. And the animals must need to drink a lot too. You've heard of Mr O'Connor, the famous engineer, the one who built that pipeline all the way out to Kalgoorlie? He drilled the bore.'

'Clever man,' said Harry. 'Terrible that he killed himself. How could anyone do that? Leaving a family bereft, too. Must have been driven mad.'

They had rejoined her parents, who were tearing morsels of bread from a loaf brought with them in a paper bag and throwing them to the swans. Weston nudged Harry and pointed with his thumb at a portly man in a white linen suit and a big straw hat. 'Look – there's the Major!'

Harry had heard stories at the boarding-house table about the zoo's director, Major Le Souef. A popular public figure, he liked to strut through his domain and play to the gallery, people said.

'You often see his children skipping around him,' Kenneth Riven had told Harry. 'Their family home is up there right next to the zoo, at the top of Yellow Hill – that two-storey stone building with the wide verandah, you've probably noticed it. The Le Souef family phaeton goes around the local streets pulled by three Shetland ponies.'

This whimsical family conveyance, someone else mentioned, had an amusing counterpart within the zoo grounds: a little carriage to which a pair of goats was harnessed would take half a dozen children at a time on rides around the oval. Other animals, too, were reportedly almost part of the family; Major Le Souef had once placed two of his babies in panniers on a donkey's back, so the story went, and led them along one of the pathways, to the great delight of the crowds.

Harry and Nellie watched now as the Major ambled along like a jovial version of the Pied Piper, a gaggle of children at his heels, and disappeared around a corner.

As Nellie's parents strolled ahead, Harry drew her attention to a glass case. 'What's this little striped thing?' He peered at the sign. 'Numbat. It's like another country here in the west, isn't it? You've got creatures I've never heard of.'

She pulled a face at the taxidermal exhibit. 'I don't like to see a stuffed animal,' she said. 'It's a horrid way to treat any creature. Everything in a zoo should be alive.'

'Yes, they should. But many of them look only half-alive here anyway. They've been turned into abject prisoners. That's what I was trying to say to your father when we saw those wretched bears.'

'Then you don't accept what he said about sub-human creatures being quite different from us in God's eyes?'

'Frankly, no – I can't think of us as being given "dominion over dumb animals", as if they're simply made to be our underlings.'

Nellie looked troubled. 'Surely humans *are* different from beasts,' she said with a frown. 'It's obvious, isn't it? They can't talk, for one thing. They can't do all sorts of things we do.'

'And we can't do some things they can do! So human beings are distinctive, I agree. Of course, yes. But the difference isn't of the kind that should entitle us to be masters of every other living thing.'

She stopped, tilting her head quizzically to one side. 'What do you believe the main difference is, Mr Hopewell?'

He tucked a thumb under his chin as he shaped an answer. 'To my mind, it's summed up in a saying that my mother likes to repeat. A little quotation from some poet – don't know who: "We look before and after, and pine for what is not." More than anything else, that's what separates people from other animals.'

She wrinkled her forehead. 'I'm not sure I understand. What does it mean to you, that saying?'

'Just that we humans don't live fully in the present, the way a lion or a pig does. A lot of the time we're preoccupied with what used to be, and what might yet happen. With remembering and imagining. That's not true of creatures in cages. I hope not, anyway – terrible for them if they have regretful or wistful feelings.'

They walked on in silence for a minute or two. He began to fret; perhaps he had been too forthright. Was she offended?

But then came a sudden commotion, heralding what Monday's newspaper headline would describe as STARTLING INCIDENT AT ZOO.

Just ahead and to their left the orangutan had somehow swung high enough on a rope to reach out and grasp the top of the fence surrounding its cage, and scramble over. It crouched on the path, tilting its head towards a fear-frozen group of children.

Nellie whimpered, and Harry put a protective hand at her back. It was the first time he had touched her, and he was acutely aware that only thin fabric separated his fingertips from her flesh. 'I don't think it can hurt us,' he told her, hoping he sounded more confident than he felt.

The creature shuffled forward, taking its weight on its fists, with the short back legs following like an afterthought. Sunlight glinted on the auburn coat and lent it a handsome sheen.

The Major came up the path towards it, neither hurrying nor hesitating, hands forward, palms open, while he repeated its name in a calm tone. 'Jenny,' he said, 'Hello Jenny.'

He kept approaching with a slow, steady gait, talking gently, until he was standing beside her. Taking off his hat and squatting down so that their heads were on a level, he put an affectionate hand on her shoulder. The gesture seemed to transform her instantly from hairy dwarf into family member. She reciprocated, draping her long thick arm around his back. Her head was bowed as if in deep thought. They leaned towards each other for a moment in the slanting afternoon sunshine, for all the world like a father and daughter tenderly exchanging confidences. Then he stood up, took her hand in his and led her back to her little compound, murmuring quiet words that none of the silent bystanders could hear. He gave her the rope. She paused for a while, apparently considering her options, and then swung across the fence, and dropped down to a platform on her climbing frame. One of the keepers ran up with a bunch of bananas to the Major, who threw them to Jenny and blew her a paternal kiss.

The crowd sighed in unison, and then began to clap. The Major lifted his hat in acknowledgement, and wandered off down a shrub-lined alley as the applause died away.

As Harry lay restlessly in bed that night, two different forms of young womanhood quivered in his imagination. In the foreground was Nellie as he wanted to think of her: demure, epitomising an ideal of graceful and maidenly decorum, as ethereally pure as her blouse was white. And partly obscured behind her there was the disturbing shape of a female body, half-naked, full-bosomed.

He knew where that more shadowy figure came from. The image had often reappeared since the day when, as a twelve-year-old boy, he'd gone next door at his mother's bidding to ask young Mrs O'Hara for some sugar.

'Explain to her I'm in the middle of making a plum cake and I've run a bit short on the caster sugar. Take this cup – that's all I need. She won't mind filling it for you. I gave her one of our lettuces a few days ago.'

So he'd gone around towards their neighbour's back door, and Mrs O'Hara was sitting on a wicker chair out in the sun, facing away from him. When he came up to her she turned, and he saw that the front of her dress was unbuttoned as she fed her baby. She didn't cover herself – just gave him a slow warm smile as she shifted the tiny mouth from one nipple to the other. He stared and felt himself flushing as he stammered out his message about the sugar.

'I'll get it for you as soon as I've finished here,' she said. He tried to look away but couldn't, and stood there awkwardly with one hand in his pocket and the other gripping the cup.

'Haven't you seen a baby suckling before?'

He shook his head. The baby began to whimper as its lips lost contact.

'It's all guzzle and grizzle at her age,' sighed Mrs O'Hara as she cupped a large pale breast with one hand and guided its darker pink-brown tip into the greedy little orifice.

Head tilted, she looked at him with an amused expression.

'Nature's way, Harry. No need to be embarrassed. But some people don't like to think about the flesh, so let's keep this to ourselves, eh?'

He nodded, scuffing his toe in the dusty grass.

And thought about it repeatedly in the months and years that followed, long after the O'Haras left the neighbourhood.

Here was that image again now, coming back to disconcert his attempts to focus on Nellie.

Sleep arrived at last, but not soothingly. His dreams were troubling. In the scene that stayed with him as he woke, Nellie turned slowly towards him with a sly smile, unbuttoned her blouse, and put a baby to her breast – but it was not quite a human child: it had the wizened face and long auburn hair of an orangutan.

Three

Above the foamy lather his eyes looked back brightly at him from the shaving mirror, and he whistled as he stropped his razor.

Since childhood, Harry had always been a merry whistler. While he worked or played, while he strolled along the street or sat reading the newspaper, his lips would purse automatically and a pure flute-like sound would keep him company. When he whistled he felt cheerful; when he felt cheerful he whistled. It had become second nature, and much of the time he was hardly conscious of what he was whistling, but his fellow workers and fellow lodgers knew well his penchant for Stephen Foster's melodies.

Right now he could hardly have been happier. It was another fine clear day, though with a mildness that freshened the air, and he was about to take Nellie out walking. Since that time at the zoo a couple of weeks before, they had talked often across the bakery counter, though briefly. He felt more at ease with her, sure she was receptive to a growing friendship. They were on first-name terms now. This would be their first excursion alone together. There were a thousand things to talk about, and above all he was keen to convey to her somehow his exhilarated sense of being full of energy, a youthful participant in this youthful twentieth century, with so many adventurous discoveries taking place and so many prospects opening on every side. It was a world that beckoned him, and he wanted her, too, to feel its allure.

As he walked along the street he was full of good cheer. He called out a greeting to old Fritz, leaning on his front fence. He waved to Freddie Dingle, coming out of the corner store. A cheeky magpie sang to him and he whistled derisively back. When he knocked at the Weston's house door, down the side path to the left of their bakery, Nellie opened it with a warm smile – and then a younger girl, all freckles and teeth, appeared at her shoulder. She looked no more than thirteen or fourteen.

'This is Doris from next door,' explained Nellie. 'Doris Biddle. Dad says she's to come along with us.' Doris beamed.

'A gooseberry!' complained Harry in a whisper to Nellie as they set off. But Doris didn't hinder them. Skipping ahead, plaits swinging beneath her bonnet, she kept to herself most of the time.

They made their way without haste, crunching underfoot the shells that the Roads Board had taken from the shore and scattered on sandy tracks through the bush to make footpaths for children wending their way to school past the boundary of the zoo.

As they strolled, Harry's enthusiasms brimmed and began to spill over into his speaking.

'This really is the most wonderful time to be alive, Nellie!' he exclaimed, his words tumbling out like a flock of pigeons released from their loft. 'I feel sure the next few years are going to keep producing new things for us to marvel at. Truly! Our lives will be more thrilling than anything people have ever experienced in the past. And more…well, more expansive, too. Just think of it: there can't be any doubt we're at the beginning of an era when mankind will take possession of the air, after thousands of years of earth-bound history.'

'Take possession?' She wrinkled her brow.

'That's what it amounts to. You've heard about all the flying machines that are being built now? Well I've watched a couple of them take off, and it won't be long, I tell you, before they become commonplace. Lifting us up. Letting us soar like birds. And wireless signals will send our messages speeding across vast distances. The possibilities are astonishing! It'll change everything. With the help of these new inventions, explorers will soon be able to venture into all the remaining uncharted corners of the world, like the Antarctic.'

'Hey!' she said, laughter dancing around the rim of her parasol. 'Slow down! One thing at a time.'

He laughed at himself, too, and gave an apologetic shrug.

'Sorry to be blurting out all of this in a rush. But there are just so many stories to tell you – things I've seen, things I want to see. And I want you to picture them, too. Those flying machines, for instance, aeroplanes…'

'So you've seen them with your own eyes? Where?'

'Not around these parts. I wish I'd witnessed that famous flight near here, at Belmont racecourse last year. Must have been spectacular! Up there for a full ten minutes – can you believe it? But it wasn't the first powered flight in Australia, you know. That came the year before, when Houdini brought a biplane with him to Melbourne, packed in crates, and flew it successfully.'

'Houdini the showman, the one who escapes from handcuffs?'

'That's him. After Melbourne he came to Sydney and I went to Rosehill to see him take off. He wasn't in the air for long, but we made ourselves hoarse cheering him like a hero. And before that, back in '09, not long before Christmas, I watched the first flight by any Australian in a machine heavier than air. Just a flimsy glider, no motor in it, but what a thing to see! George Taylor and his wife, each of them in turn, made flight after flight over the sand. I'll never forget the thrill of it. I wish you could have been there, Nellie.'

Pausing, Harry entered again into the dreamy sensation he had so often imagined since that day: he too was in flight, skimming over the sand, feeling the vibration through his hands as they gripped the struts, seeing flashes of sunlight on the water out there; and everything was eerily silent except for the whoosh beneath his wings as invisible currents uplifted him and he slipped and slid across the airy sibilant pathways.

The trance dissolved and he went on talking. 'A moment in history – and it took place not far from where I lived! Our home was in Collaroy, you see. Anyway, word got around that the Taylors were preparing for a controlled flight at Narrabeen Heads, next beach along. So I borrowed our neighbour's bicycle and pedalled furiously. I had a marvellous view of it all.'

'Must have been entertaining. But you don't really think ordinary people will ever want to climb into those dangerous machines?' She curled a ringlet around her finger.

'Well, in the near future, I reckon, it won't be dangerous.' Loosening his collar, he wiped the sweat away from his neck with the back of his hand. 'It'll be an everyday event. And it'll be about much more than entertainment, Nellie. Aeroplanes are soon going to become less flimsy, more reliable, no doubt about it. They'll travel further and capture everyone's attention. Lots of people will learn to be pilots – I fervently hope to be one of them! – and lots of others are going to line up to be passengers, or send cargo, because flying will simply be the most efficient way to cover big distances, I'm sure of it. Someone who's only looking for entertainment can do the usual things, like visiting a circus or a zoo.'

'I thought you enjoyed yourself at the zoo,' she said with a reproachful moue.

'Yes, yes, it was fun. Of course. Going anywhere with you would be fun, Nellie. But a zoo...well, it doesn't contribute anything to progress, does it?'

She seemed to be thinking that over. Or perhaps she was bored.

'I've been talking too much,' he said contritely. 'I didn't intend to.'

'I like listening to you.'

He began to whistle a slow tune.

'That's very familiar,' she said, 'but I can't think of the name.'

'"Beautiful Dreamer".'

'Of course.'

They smiled shyly at each other.

The day was heating up. The path had taken them up to a crest, where they found a patch of shade beside a clump of she-oaks and took their ease as they looked down to the Como foreshore. Harry removed his hat.

'Your hair is the same colour as a lion's coat,' said Nellie. He blushed and made no response. Could she be thinking, as he was, of that scene of nonchalant copulation at the zoo?

Lethargic, they chattered idly, brushing the flies away. Doris held a piece of grass between her thumbs and blew on it to produce a raucous vibrato. A wattlebird rebuked her from a bush nearby and Doris threw a shell at it.

Voices drifted towards them in a singsong tone. Then two men with coolie hats appeared around a turn in the track, jabbering to each other until they saw they were not alone. As they approached with a shuffling gait, side by side, legs moving together as if in a three-legged race, they grinned broadly and nodded continuously. 'Goo' day, ni' day,' said one of them, and the other echoed his greeting. All smiles, they passed by.

Harry had seen Chinamen toiling away in their bamboo-fringed market gardens down on the swampy stretch of riverside to the east of his boarding house, planting, hoeing, carrying water, clearing the ditches that criss-crossed the vegetable plots. Sometimes in the evenings you could hear twangly instrumental music coming from their little shanties, and vocal noise that was half-gabbling and half-giggling. Seemed to enjoy themselves all right.

Doris wrinkled her nose as she watched the pair receding into the distance. 'They give me the creeps, those Ching-Chongs,' she said. Harry was taken aback.

'They do no harm, Doris,' he said. 'And they're hard workers.'

'But they're so... They're just like monkeys.'

'That's a bit harsh,' Harry remonstrated. 'We probably seem as strange to them as they do to us.'

Shaking her head, Doris turned to Nellie. 'Horrible, aren't they?'

Nellie frowned. 'They look different, but I don't really know anything about them. When I asked my dad once what they're like and why they'd have left China to come here, he just said, "Don't waste your curiosity on heathens". What do you think, Harry? Do they have the same feelings we do?'

'Who knows? I suppose lots of white people feel things differently from one another.'

'But Chinamen just don't belong in our country,' said Doris sulkily. 'They're pests!'

'Hardly,' said Harry. 'It's not as if they're overrunning us. You can try putting them behind a big fence if they ever get as numerous here as rabbits – but that won't happen.'

The afternoon sun was beginning to drop in the brazen sky. 'I'm tired,' whimpered Doris. 'Shouldn't we be going home?'

'Quite right, young lady,' said Harry, standing up and swinging his arms vigorously as if they were a pair of propellers. He put his hand under Nellie's elbow and helped her to her feet.

As they sauntered back along the sandy track, Nellie asked him about his family.

'I'm an only child, like you,' he told her. Having that in common, he thought, might partly explain why he felt confident that he understood so much about her: conscious of being both solitary and surrounded, of being the focus of a family's expectation – she must be shaped by that constant awareness, just as he surely was himself.

'What are they like, your parents?' she asked. 'Are they strict, the way mine are?'

'Not really. More indulgent, I'd say. My parents made me feel I was the centre of the family. I remember Mum telling me with smile, when I was very young, "You're the apple of your dad's eye, you know. And of mine too, son." To a little boy it seemed a strange saying, but it obviously meant something good because she looked so pleased and loving when she said it.'

'They must be happy you turned out so clever.'

'I don't know about clever. High-spirited was what they used to say. They've expected me to work hard. Both of them had to leave school by the time they were thirteen, but they were proud of their few skills, and keen for me to acquire more knowledge than they had. "Always try to better yourself, Harry", Mum used to say.'

He could still hear her voice in his head: 'Look at your dad, now. Didn't get much schooling, but he used to practise his sums, practise, practise. So now he can run his eye quickly over a column of numbers and add them up just like that, in his head. And his penmanship! He wrote such nice letters to me – they weren't very long, but he had a handsome hand.'

A handsome hand: being just a young lad when she told him that, Harry had been struck by the expression and used to stare at his father's great paws with their thick heavy-knuckled fingers, puzzled that his mother liked the look of them.

He thought now of the slow way his father always spoke, assaying the weight of each phrase, deliberating, looking both ways, chiding his son affectionately for rushing headlong into things like a bull at a gate: *Hurried Harold*, he would sometimes call him, smiling to soften the rebuke, and at other times *Harry-in-a-hurry*.

'I get a little letter from home every week,' he told Nellie. 'Dad writes half a page in his neat copperplate, and Mum adds a few sentences. Not much news, but they tell me what's growing in the garden, or describe the cat's antics, or any changes in the area – houses going up, the new electric tramway link that's planned for Narrabeen, things like that. And I write back and let them know what it's like living here and how the job is going. I've told them about you, too.'

Her sudden smile was like a shaft of light.

They were descending a steep part of the track in single file when there was a little cry and Nellie fell forward, sprawling beside him. As he stooped to help her up, he tried not to stare at the bare leg, pale and slim, exposed by her rucked-up skirt.

'No, not hurt,' she said in response to his anxious query. 'Just a slight graze on my knee.' He glimpsed it as she straightened the skirt. 'I'll put some ointment on it as soon as I get home. Clumsy of me – I must have tripped on that tree root there.'

'Would you like to lean on my arm as we walk?'

'Thank you, but no need – I feel fine.'

For days afterwards, as he went about his tasks at the station on the hill, he kept picturing her pale leg, wanting to stroke it. The word *caress* lingered in his thoughts.

Four

When he next went to the bakery counter, it was Nellie's father who served him.

'Like to join us for a meal on Friday evening?' Weston asked casually. 'There'll be a good hearty roast dinner.'

So it was arranged. On the dot, Harry came up the path whistling quietly and resolving to curb his natural loquacity. But that resolution was soon forgotten when Weston plied him with questions about the station project.

'This wireless idea – what's the point of it?'

Harry took a deep breath. 'Well, you see, it's going to allow people to do things they've never been able to do before. Important things. Until recent years it hasn't been possible to communicate quickly with anyone beyond ordinary hearing range. Out of earshot meant out of immediate contact.'

'So we have a postal service,' said Weston with a shrug.

'Yes, but writing and sending letters can take a long while. Then just a few decades ago, as you know, inventors found a way of sending messages along telegraph cables with no lapse of time – but only between the points at either end of the cable, and it's much the same with telephones. So here's the great thing about wireless: it isn't restricted like that. It transmits signals that anyone can pick up anywhere – well, almost anywhere – if they have the right apparatus, with special valves. So in the future, the near future, we'll be able to send our words rushing through the ether from one part of the world to another. They'll travel on our behalf without the need for cables. Miraculous, isn't it?'

'Puts my head in a spin,' said Nellie.

'I still don't see,' said her father, 'why the government wants to put a wireless station here. Who needs it?'

Swallowing a stubborn piece of gristle, Harry put down his knife and fork and wiped his mouth.

'For one thing,' he explained patiently, 'wireless can make our whole country a lot safer. Now that we're a federation, not just a scatter of separate colonies, there's a long national boundary to monitor, isn't there? Australia's such a whopping great island that invaders could easily come ashore in many places. And at first hardly anyone would even know it had happened. Wireless stations around the coast can protect us in the future, you see, by communicating with naval vessels and with other stations. Wireless will be a boon to merchant shipping, too. And before long there'll be a lot of other uses. Sending the latest news from place to place, for example. Instantaneously.'

'But I don't really understand what wireless is,' Nellie confessed. 'Exactly how it works, I mean.'

'Well, let's see. You need a transmitter at one end of the process, and that's part of what we're building now on the hill at Applecross. It's a machine for turning sounds – Morse code signals, or perhaps even speech before long – into waves, electromagnetic waves, that can be sent through the air with the help of an aerial mast, an antenna – so we're constructing one of those too. And then at the receiving end, on a ship at sea for instance, there has to be another machine that will turn those waves back into sound again…'

Weston frowned. 'What's this code you're talking about?'

'Morse code? Oh it's a clever way of communicating over big distances without needing to use words. A bit like an alphabet, but it's made up of electrical pulses – a rhythmic sequence of short and long pulses. Each letter has a corresponding pattern of dots and dashes – short and long sounds. So for example if you convert Nellie's name into Morse code it starts with a dash followed by a dot – that's the 'N', you see – and then there's a single dot to represent the 'E', and a dot dash dot dot sequence for the 'L', and so on.'

'Hmm. Must be hard to remember. How did you learn about all these technical things?'

'I got interested in engineering as a schoolboy, Mr Weston. Though to begin with that wasn't where my interests mainly tended, as a matter of fact. At an early age, mainly from my parents, I'd picked up an enthusiasm for words. Their shades of meaning, their power to cast a spell. And so poetry and stories fascinated me. When I was still quite little I used to tell people I intended to write books when I grew up.'

Weston gave a sceptical sniff, and his wife looked bemused by the outlandish notion of shaded meaning, but Harry pushed on.

'Then when I was about ten or eleven I had teacher, Meredith Moon, who was a great exponent of science – a bit of an eccentric, very shy, squeaky little voice behind walrus whiskers, but he had a gift for explaining things. He used to bring along a couple of magazines, *Popular Mechanics* and *Scientific American*, and read the articles to us in class. And I picked up whatever I could from my own reading, too. Started to keep a scrapbook of newspaper clippings and pamphlets. Reports from overseas about brilliant inventors, that fellow Marconi especially – what a genius! And there were some enterprising people in Sydney at the time, trying to develop more powerful transmission... I'm not boring you, I hope?'

'No, no,' said Nellie quickly. 'Tell us more.'

So he rattled on about the group in Randwick run by Brother Placid, the Wireless Priest, and how he watched them put up a backyard steel tower for sending messages to their Pacific Island missions. Told them, too, about his own training as a wireless engineer at the technical college in Ultimo, and about his good fortune when one of the college lecturers saw how enthusiastic he was and asked him to join a new company, Australasian Wireless Limited.

AWL, Harry explained, was linked to the big German company, Telefunken, and had just won a government contract to build a couple of wireless stations, one in Sydney at Pennant Hills and the other on the Applecross site. He'd luckily been given the task of installing the power unit at both places – 'And I haven't looked back,' he added.

'So where will this lead you after the station's built?' Weston asked. 'Is there some sort of career ahead in this wireless business? A steady job?'

'There'll be openings for someone with my kind of experience, certainly,' Harry assured him. 'The government wants to build more stations up the coast, and I reckon other opportunities will turn up.'

By the time the dishes were cleared and Mrs Weston took up her knitting, Harry felt he had probably passed the test of provisional acceptability. Though Nellie's parents didn't seem particularly warm towards him, he supposed this just reflected their habitual reticence. They might be puzzled or doubtful about his work as an electrical engineer, but nothing he said had incurred disapproval, as far as he could tell. And while he'd been wary about the possibility of putting a foot wrong if they'd brought up any religious topics, to his relief it hadn't happened.

When the conversation began to peter out, he thanked them for their hospitality and stood up to leave.

'Oh – I nearly forgot.' Harry pulled a news clipping from his pocket. 'This is from yesterday's paper. There's another evening concert coming up at the zoo, weekend after next. Here's what it says: *The same quartet that performed so well on the last occasion will return to the Zoological Gardens on Saturday 9th March. The grounds will be illuminated with hundreds of candles in Chinese lanterns and many-coloured hanging glass jars. The organising committee promises that patrons will be charmed by this 'rainbow radiance' and by the aromatic flowerbeds, ornamental ponds and rockeries, and gushing fountains.* I'm hoping Nellie can come with me to the concert,' he said, turning to her parents. 'If she'd like to, I mean. And with your permission, of course.'

There was an exchange of nods.

The following Friday he woke with a fever, a swollen throat, and a sense of bitter disappointment. Going to Saturday's concert was out of the question, but he had bought the tickets in advance, a shilling each, and it would be a shame to waste them. He persuaded Mrs Riven to take the tickets along to Weston's bakery with a note urging Nellie to use them: young Doris Biddle, he suggested, would surely be glad to go to the concert with her.

It took several days until Harry felt well enough to return to work. Before walking to the ferry he called in at the bakery, hoping to hear what Nellie thought of the concert. But her father told him she was indisposed herself now, and would need to stay in bed for a while.

When he next saw Nellie, more than a week after the concert, she looked wan, a little out of sorts – still convalescing, presumably.

'You're not quite yourself yet,' he'd said solicitously. She only shook her head and changed the subject. A few days later he got cross with her because he discovered she'd withheld something from him. Although their near-quarrel was quickly over, as the weeks slipped by there were a few times when he thought he might perhaps have offended her somehow. No, she'd said, when he asked – nothing wrong. Just a bit off colour, that was all.

But the very last time he saw Nellie she was in a strange mood, downcast or distracted, and the way she spoke to him on that occasion was all the more painful because the family's mysterious disappearance came so soon afterwards.

How fragile, he now knew, a seemingly sturdy contentment can turn out to be; how quickly the most ebullient emotions can sink into despondency.

Every working morning for months now he had made the little journey from South Perth through the Narrows and round into Melville Water, past Point Dundas to the far end of Lucky Bay, leaning at the rail, watching the scrubby shoreline slide past with its dark scribble of banksias and she-oaks, and feeling the wind on his face. There was nearly always wind, even at that hour, and by the time he headed homeward it had usually freshened from the west. On each river trip, to and fro, thoughts of Nellie had drifted through his mind – cheerfully for the first few months, fretfully since her vanishing. This morning the dolphins were cavorting beside the boat again. Not long ago their antics would have made him grin with pleasure, but now, subdued in spirit, he had just stared at them blankly.

They used to talk a lot about the river, Nellie and he. Her memories of family picnics beside the little inlet known as Miller's Pool had charmed him. She made it sound such a delightful place that he insisted on walking along Suburban Road with her (and the ever-attendant Doris) to see it. As she reminisced, he could see how Miller's Pool – just a shallow basin, really, with a small opening into the river – must have been a haven, a place of delight for children who wanted somewhere to fish, or to sail their model boats along its small sheltered beach, or to collect shells after school and at weekends. Some local residents used to keep their dinghies moored in the shelter of the pool. One of them, said Nellie, was the mayor of South Perth, who lived at Mill Point and regularly rowed across to Perth and back.

Fish were plentiful in the Swan, she told him, and not only fish. On summer evenings there were groups clustered here and there along the riverbank, each with its little fire on the sand, having supper from buckets of cooked prawns and crabs that they had caught just by wading out with nets.

She told him what she knew about the place and its history.

'My dad says that before the land around here was divided up for home sites, the small boats – *flats*, I think they called them – would come in to deliver sacks of grain from Guildford or Fremantle to the old mill over there.' She pointed to a stumpy remnant, its blades gone, with a half-derelict cottage beside it. 'And collect flour from it too. Doesn't look much now, does it, all bedraggled? – but they say it's the oldest pair of buildings in the Perth area. So this spot must have been settled a long time back, seventy or eighty years Dad reckons. There were blacks earlier on, of course, already here when the pioneers arrived. But they didn't do anything, apparently, except a bit of fishing and walking around. Nowadays they spend their time in a camp they've set up near the Causeway, along there to the east – know where I mean?'

He remembered pointing out to Nellie how the role of the river was changing. He enjoyed explaining things, showing off a bit. She seemed to like listening.

'In the early days,' he told her, 'the Swan must have been almost the only way the settlers could get around. Different now, isn't it? Roads and railways are already starting to take over from the river, you can see that. We won't always rely on ferries and barges. Before long, mark my words, this stretch of water will be used mainly for pleasure craft, yachting regattas, things like that. Oh there'll always be the fishing, too, and prawning and crabbing along the shore. But when manufacturing gets cheaper and the roads improve with asphalt paving, you'll see big changes – lots more bicycles, automobiles, trams, trucks. There's even talk of building a bridge one day across the Narrows. And people will get around the suburbs on wheels. Imagine it, Nellie: instead of using a horse and cart for delivering your bread, you'll have a motor van!'

She had chuckled softly at such an absurd idea. The forlorn memory of her laughter gnawed at him now. Would he ever hear that lilting sound again?

Five

Pausing near the top of the blackened hillside, he turned to look down at the distant river. Even with eyelids half-closed against the glare and the flies, he had a clear view of the broad expanse of water, wind-ruffled, stretching right across to the dark grey-green hogsback of King's Park.

From the small ridge he stood on, most of the region surrounding Perth looked dismally level, its horizontal monotony broken by little more than a few sandy mounds. The contrast with his home city and its outlying townships could hardly be greater. There was nothing here comparable to the breathtaking steepness of his home street in Collaroy. Everything in and near Sydney jutted up and out, this way or that, always feeling firm underfoot: the land was compacted into clods of clay or huge lumps of rock. Here, instead of those solid foundations and sharp angles there were just soft accumulations of limestone grit, mostly flat but sometimes swelling and sloping into dunes that looked like stationary waves.

Around him the wireless station site was featureless, bald as a plucked fowl: trees felled, scrub burnt, shade all gone, nothing higher than an inch above the ground anywhere on the crest or slopes except for the new buildings. Did they really need to clear all the vegetation so completely?

This morning he had disembarked at the usual place at the usual time and trudged up the new curving asphalt road to the crest of the ridge, but it was hard to settle to any work knowing the rest of the equipment was due to arrive imminently. Now, as the barge approached, he made his way back down the hill and across Fremantle Road towards the new jetty with Max and Sven and the Public Works gang. German Jetty they called it, because the sole purpose of building it had been to provide a place for bringing the heavy pieces of Telefunken machinery ashore.

They were well prepared for the arrival of this equipment. The Engine House had been ready for a while and the mast was up and waiting. With the final bit of the rig coming into position just a week before, Max Schank's pride had been plain to see as the cheers rang out around him. The team had all gathered near the base of the mast, with its bed of thick glass insulation plates that made Harry think of a stack of his mother's pikelets, magnified and shiny. Schank stood looking up admiringly at the great latticed steel aerial, his feet planted apart, hands on heavy hips, elbows out, his head seeming about to topple off the back of his thick neck as he strained to see the topmost point.

'Hey, it's a bloody big bodkin, isn't it?' he said.

And more than that. To Harry's mind it suggested several familiar things fantastically elongated. He saw it as a kind of elegant silver pencil for inscribing ciphered messages on an ethereal medium. Or as a magical cloud-capped beanstalk ladder like the one in the folktale he remembered his dad recounting with fee-fi-fo-fum gusto. Or even as a spire: aspiring, rising grandly from earth to sky, seeming to stand for so much of the spirit of this new age, this era of marvellous achievement and boundless promise.

For a moment he could almost forget about the painful mystery of Nellie's absence. Today's main task was unloading in sections the massive power unit shipped over from Germany. This, above all, was what the company had brought Harry here to work on, and he knew exactly what it would comprise because it was so similar to the one he installed in Sydney and he'd studied every detail of the diagrams closely: a semi-diesel Gardner engine, 75 horsepower, with a flywheel and split pulley. It was his responsibility to assemble the sections and get the whole unit securely bolted to the concrete pad so that with a thick leather belt it could drive a 500-volt generator and a 10,000-volt transformer – 'the monsters', as he called them affectionately – which were already in position.

The Public Works supervisor had procured a hefty steam traction engine for the day's work. It took nearly three hours of sweaty effort with ropes, rollers and pulleys to manoeuvre the components from the barge to the jetty and then, load by load, onto a trolley; and most of the rest of the day for the traction engine, on four separate runs, to haul the trolley up to the top of the hill, huffing continually and stalling frequently.

Much of the next day would be spent dragging each part inside the building and into position there. Harry stood at the door of the generator room, sobered by the thought that achieving transmission would soon be almost entirely in his hands. It ought to be straightforward, once all the assembling work was done. The quenched spark transmitter was reliable, he felt sure – an efficient, unspectacular device, with just a faint sizzling sound as the power surged. He half-wished he could witness the more dramatic display that the outmoded Marconi system produced, if their Chief Engineer Martin van der Sluis was to be believed: he'd been on hand, he told them, for the first American transmission across the Atlantic, at a station Marconi built on Cape Cod.

'Astonishing sight! When this contraption fired off its discharge there was a crackling flash of bluish sparks. You'd think thunder and lightning had burst into the next room.'

None of them doubted the significance of the work they were doing. A sturdy coastal wireless system would change lives, save lives. That shocking disaster back in April, the loss of the *Titanic*: terrible that so many perished, but without a wireless operator on board to send distress signals to other ships the hundreds who were plucked alive from the water would have drowned too, and the *Titanic* would have been just another mysterious disappearance – like the *Koombana* up the Western Australian coast the month before that, sinking without a trace somewhere out from Port Hedland, and so many people on board, about 140 the papers said, with not one survivor. If only there had been wireless communication between ship and shore they could have called for help.

'Never heard of Richardson's big ride? Let me tell you, young fellas: don't get starry-eyed about those groups of Englishmen and Norwegians racing each other towards the South Pole. The newspapers pay them a lot of attention, and you can say what you like about their bravery. Don't forget, though, they've got plenty of money and equipment behind them, support teams, all of that. Yeah, must be colder than the grave in that godforsaken place, but you don't have to go to the far corners of the earth to find bloody impressive examples of rugged men braving tough conditions. And for the best of them it's a solo effort! Now here's why you oughta know about Arthur Richardson.'

Freddie Dingle leaned forward, jabbing at the air with his pipe as he spoke. The rest of the construction gang sat in a circle around him, listening, smiling, smoking, sipping tea from their enamel mugs and shooing the flies away. Harry, responsive to any tale of heroic achievement and curious about what made Freddie tick, leaned against the doorframe, absorbing every word.

'He was the first bloke to ride a bicycle across the Nullarbor, y'see, and he did it on his pat in scorching summer weather, too. This was back in '96. Took nothing with him but a small kit and a waterbag. He followed the telegraph line, and you can bet there was a lot of sweating and swearing on the gritty roads. He arrived in Adelaide on Christmas Day just a month after leaving Coolgardie. Amazing.'

Harry could picture it all – the chafed skin, the desert winds, mile after mile of featureless sandhills.

'But that's not all,' Freddie went on. 'Blow me down, less than three years later the bugger was at it again, pedalling round the whole bloody continent! No-one had done that before. It's all in his book, *Story of a Remarkable Ride* it's called. You blokes oughta get hold of a copy. Damn good story. I was in the crowd that gave him a send-off. He left Perth in mid-winter, heading up clockwise, carrying just a bit of luggage and a pistol. Well, he made slow progress because of heavy rain, y'see, and for long distances he had to carry his bike. Up north there were hostile blacks to contend with, and food was a bit of a problem at times, but he made his way right across the top into Queensland, then on down, and back westwards. By the time he hit the Nullabor it was fierce heat again. Got back to Perth in February, after eight months and eleven-and-a-half thousand bloody miles!

'Then after just a few weeks, what does he do? Sets off from Fremantle for the South African War. And how d'you like this? – he takes a bike along with him! Off to war on a bike, donated by some local shopkeeper for him to use as a whaddya call it, dispatch rider. Never heard what became of him after that. He's probably riding across the Sahara bloody Desert trying to beat a camel team to the next oasis!'

There were chuckles all round. Everyone liked to hear Freddie Dingle's yarns. He was the heart, belly and mouth of the Public Works team. They seemed to enjoy the way he teased them, taunted them. His gritty, rasping voice sounded like wet cement being shovelled out of a wheelbarrow. He coined mildly disparaging nicknames for most of the men. But Harry, whose honey curls and air of confident candour turned him inevitably into 'Goldilocks', felt sure that Freddie's gruff chiacking was just a coarse blanket pulled protectively over other qualities. For all the roughness of his manner, Freddie kept a close eye on his workmates. When the news got around that Nellie had vanished it was Freddie who put a sympathetic hand on Harry's shoulder and spoke to him quietly. There was something anxious in him too, even vulnerable. Although his body was as thick as a wool bale, his fingernails were chewed into vestiges.

'Aargh, Freddie,' scoffed Max Schank with a smile that tempered the raillery, 'vee know vy you make a hero of this mad dog Richardson. You vant to skite about your own daily feats of bike riding between home and verk.'

Some of the men sniggered. They all knew that Freddie was trying to keep his weight down by pedalling and puffing all the way each morning from South Perth, where he lived along the street from Harry, to Applecross and then back again at the end of the day.

They were a motley crew, thought Harry as he looked around at these fellows he worked with: several nationalities, temperaments as different as the colours on a patchwork quilt, but they were all engaged on a shared task whose by-product was a rough kind of tolerance, even respect, achieved through jokes and banter and a sense of the value of what they were creating together. They had converged on this little corner of Western Australia from other states, other countries, and in their collaborative endeavour Harry believed he could glimpse the world of tomorrow, when wireless – along with aeroplanes and other new inventions – would help to remove the barriers between different peoples, different places. He saw with his inward eye a planet encircled by waves, not only in the constant rhythmic undulation of mighty expanses of water but also in the pulsing and rippling relay of electromagnetic signals, invisible, miraculously rapid.

It was now nearly a month since she had slipped away into baffling silence. Composing letters to her in his head during quiet interludes at work or long evenings in his room at the boarding house gave him some solace, as if she were still somehow in reach of his words.

Dearest Nellie, I miss your smile and long for your return... (Would that seem too ardent?)

When you come back, there are so many things I want us to do together... (Perhaps a bit suggestive?)

Do you like the idea of a picnic at Point Walter? It has become a very popular spot for groups and couples on Saturdays... He tried to picture her stepping with him onto the jetty there, reaching for his hand to steady herself, sunlight glittering on the water behind them, her face happy under her white bonnet. They would be talking without shyness, and their shared future would expand.

He remembered the words he had quoted that time at the zoo. *We look before and after, and pine for what is not.*

Six

It failed the test. The suspense had stretched them taut, and the let-down deflated them. After all the effort expended on this project, after all the time and money and excited hopes, the wireless reception wasn't working properly.

Harry took it most to heart. Solving the problem was up to him. Word got around the group quickly, and smoke-oh that morning was quieter than usual. Harry didn't join the others. He sat staring glumly at the huge switchboard behind the generating unit and tried to think what to do. Flynn the garrulous sparky approached and began to murmur some platitude but Harry shook his head and waved him away. It wasn't a time for talking.

They all knew exactly what the government contract stipulated: wireless operators at the Applecross station must be able to communicate with Sydney in daylight and with a ship 500 miles out to sea. But it now turned out that they couldn't pick up signals over those distances. It seemed likely that the weakness was in the German receiver. The crystal was simply not sensitive enough. What to do?

Harry was well aware that the Pennant Hills station would soon be ready, and officially begin its work in August. The one here in Applecross was scheduled to open in September with all requirements met, so he had six weeks at the most to get the receiver working. It was urgent to find a crystal of the best quality for the purpose. Everything he'd read or heard on the subject made him fairly sure this would be galena. He took his advice to the boss, van der Sluis, who said he'd make enquiries. A fortnight later they obtained a dark silvery piece from a small mining settlement north of Geraldton, on the Murchison River. Holding it in his hand, Harry admired the smooth shiny bevelling. It gave him a saturnine wink.

But he needed more than a suitable crystal. Bit by bit, with some adroit scrounging, he devised other makeshift components. He mounted a small insulator on a breadboard base. Then, taking a needle that Dottie Crump had grudgingly donated from her sewing kit, he fixed its point so that a length of springy copper held it in tension and pressed it against the galena crystal, which was kept in position by a chipped cup filched from the Rivens' kitchen. This strange apparatus, improbably blending the homespun and the adamantine, worked perfectly.

Van der Sluis called the whole group together. 'Young Harry here,' he told them, grinning with relief, 'has produced a real masterpiece of improvisation.' ('Gdonya, Goldilocks!' interjected Dingle.) 'Thanks to our ingenious colleague,' the Chief continued, 'Australia's coastal defence system has been secured – with a darning needle, a breadboard and a teacup! Hail to Harry the inventor! Hip hip hooray…' As the chorus of jubilation rang across the hillside, Harry thought they must sound like a family of laughing jackasses. He revelled in the moment.

That evening, Harry went again to the police building at the corner of Mends Street and Labouchere Road. He had been dropping in there once a week to ask Tom Torrence about progress with the Weston case, hoping his regular visits would keep the police diligent. For a while Harry had thought he must be under suspicion himself, because Torrence would take out his notebook and go through the same set of questions each time, as if trying to catch him in some contradiction. Exactly when and where did he last see Nellie? She'd seemed a bit unhappy, had she? Unhappy with him? Was there some quarrel? And what about her parents – would Harry say he was on good terms with them both?

But lately Torrence had put no questions to him, and no information had emerged except a doubtful report from the night-cart man, always shickered, who said he thought he might perhaps have seen a couple of people – maybe women, maybe not, couldn't recall – walking along one of the back streets with heavy bags in the wee small hours, probably about the time when the family went missing, but he wasn't sure he hadn't dreamt it.

'Nah – no news,' Torrence told Harry with a sigh that turned into a mucous rattle. 'Drawn a blank with enquiries about rail passengers, both the Kalgoorlie line and the Albany one. No definite sightings reported. And nothing's come to light about financial problems.' He lowered his voice. 'Between ourselves, I can tell you one thing. We did find that

George Weston drew all the money from his bank account just before the disappearance. Seems clear their departure was planned – but as for why they left and where they were heading, no clues.'

Torrence sharpened his pencil and admired its point. 'So the case has come to a standstill,' he added. 'Might never be solved. Thing is, we don't even know if anything untoward happened. Seems they musta just wanted to leave town quietly. Some private reason. No law against that.'

Harry walked dejectedly down Mends Street and out along the jetty. Moonless, with a cool gusty wind, the evening was as drab as his mood. Across the river the dull light of gas lamps sketched out feebly the lines of Perth's main streets. Nellie might perhaps be over there somewhere, or much further afield. How could he begin to search for her?

He thought again about the last time he had seen her, just a few days before the disappearance. She seemed to be in an odd state of mind, withdrawn, preoccupied. When he said so, she snapped at him and they argued. It was only the second occasion there had been any cross word between them. The first came earlier, when he discovered she had not spent that Saturday evening with Doris Biddle at the zoo concert. It wasn't so much the fact of her going there alone – which he could understand, once the circumstances were clear. No, the vexing thing was that Nellie had withheld information from him for no apparent reason. In talking about the concert she had let him think that Doris did accompany her as expected. Why?

He wouldn't even have known about it if he hadn't chanced to see Doris at the corner store nearly a fortnight after the concert and asked whether she'd enjoyed her outing.

'Oh, haven't you heard, then? – I missed out,' said Doris. 'It was just so, so disappointing. I came down sick, a real bellyache, and at the last minute I wasn't allowed to go, so one of the tickets was wasted, such a pity. But Nellie went anyway – not telling Mr and Mrs Weston she was going on her own, because they would have stopped her too. Didn't Nellie explain all this?'

Harry went straight to the bakery and when Nellie started to greet him at the counter he cut her short. Why had she kept quiet, he wanted to know, about having gone alone to the zoo concert? Flushing, she replied defensively that she just didn't think it was worth mentioning it to him. Going there on her own wasn't her plan, she reminded him sharply. There was no-one else to go with – her parents had arranged to run a Christian Endeavour meeting that evening, and if she'd told them that Doris couldn't accompany her they'd have made her go along to their boring meeting instead. And anyway, why was he using that cross tone with her? Was it her fault both he and Doris were ill? Wasn't he pleased that she'd used one of the tickets he bought, and been able to listen to the lovely music?

'So you didn't meet anyone else there?'

'An assignation? Of course not!' She was indignant. 'Don't be ridiculous!'

'Just seems odd you didn't tell me you'd gone by yourself. And not very prudent to be out at an evening event with no escort.'

'But I didn't want to miss the concert,' she protested, looking hurt. 'You'd paid for me to go. Do you think I wanted to go alone? You're being unfair.'

He had sighed and shrugged. And that was all there was to their first tiff. The second one, just before her disappearance, was even briefer and yet more disturbing because he didn't know what lay behind it. He had arranged to take her to Stidworthy's tearooms on his afternoon off. During the short walk there from the bakery he talked in his usual sprightly manner about the progress he'd made with his part of the wireless station project. It was only when they had been sitting at their table for a while that he noticed how pale she was, how quiet, how disengaged. Usually she would hang on his words.

'You seem to be in a sort of reverie,' he said.

'Hmm? Oh, sorry.'

'Anything wrong?'

'Just tired.'

'You're not even eating your scones.'

'Don't feel very hungry.'

Silence settled on her again. Was she sulking over something? He couldn't imagine what. Then he made the mistake of using the word 'inattentive' and she reacted peevishly, flinging the word back at him.

'Inattentive! You're not a schoolmaster in front of a class! It's you who should pay more attention. If you did, you'd see that I don't feel up to conversation at the moment.'

'But...'

'No, please, I won't talk about it. I just want to go home.' He was startled to see there were tears glistening in her eyes.

They walked back in silence, parting awkwardly at the door – and that was the last he had seen of her.

⌒

Nearly a year after her disappearance, here he was in Geraldton. It felt to Harry like the end of the earth: Perth was remote enough, and this town was three hundred bleak and dusty miles north of Perth. The pay was good, but the job had nothing else going for it. Necessary work, no doubt, but unexciting. Now that AWL had merged with the Marconi Company to become Amalgamated Wireless Australasia, the dispute about patent ownership was no longer distracting their construction of transmitters. With the two long-range stations operating smoothly in Applecross and Pennant Hills, he'd been sent north with Sven and Max to install other parts of what the government was calling its Coastal Radio Service – smaller operations with 5 kilowatt transmitters, to be used just for communicating with ships. After Geraldton there would be Broome, Roebourne, Wyndham and Darwin, all desolate places, people said; and he'd be needed at every bloody one of them.

The work in Geraldton was slow, the heat relentless, and there was no efficient coordination of effort on the site. In fact, Harry couldn't see much effort being expended at all. The labourers from the Public Works Department were slouching layabouts. Each of them had a waterbag, filled every morning at the brewery nearby – not always with water. Sven and Max were working on the mast, though without excitement; its modest scale presented no challenge. The transmission equipment had arrived but until the building was ready for its installation Harry could do little, and having to twiddle his thumbs in this unlovely town made him tetchy.

In the early mornings, for want of anything else to do, he strode along the dismal streets and down to the long jetty where fishermen unloaded their glinting catch while strident seagulls yawled and snarled. Then he would walk aimlessly back through the town again, sometimes to the outskirts where the Afghan camel drivers clustered. Wherever he went, hardly anything warranted a second glance. The newly completed Geraldton Club building looked impressive enough, with its oval windows and corner tower, but it wasn't for the likes of him. The parapets and pediments in the main street didn't seem to belong to a place like this. Perhaps the railway station would give the town a focus eventually, but the process of constructing it, as far as Harry could see, was desultory and piecemeal: pipes and drains and coal bins half-finished, a couple of big sheds and a turntable, timber lying around, piles of gravel, not much activity.

He had no more than a vague idea of what lay inland. He'd heard that you'd soon find yourself in a landscape of withering indifference, untrodden and vast, that seemed to stretch endlessly towards a horizon where hopes shifted away, dissolved, then reappeared only to vanish again.

In the letters that came from his parents these days there was an undertow of sadness. He got the impression that their uneventful world had begun to close in on them: his father, though still in his fifties, seemed to be ailing – some unspecified problem with his lungs – and was no longer in regular employment, while his mother had apparently resigned herself to a small set of domestic routines. The experiences she mentioned were mainly vicarious: morsels of news about her sister Muriel's family in Broken Hill or things that a few neighbours and friends were doing. He felt a flicker of guilt at having been so far away from them for so long. 'You're the apple of his eye, son. And of mine too.' They had encouraged him to seize the opportunity of the wireless work and the move westward, but he supposed they must miss his company acutely. And it struck him for the first time that he missed their company, too, and missed Collaroy, not so much its village as the curving nook of coast that had sheltered and shaped his boyhood. Over here, on the rim of a gigantic ocean that stretched out to the setting of the sun, he had begun to feel stranded and friendless.

Suddenly one morning there she was, some distance ahead along the street, walking briskly away from him. She was bareheaded and he recognised her hair: the russet colour, the satin-like sheen, the soft fall of the familiar tresses against the back of her neck. He called out to her but she didn't seem to hear, hurrying on and turning down a side street. He ran to the corner and called out again, more urgently: 'Nellie!' She half-glanced back and increased her pace. Running up behind her, he drew alongside, reached out a hand – and as she looked at him apprehensively he saw at once that it was not Nellie, nothing like her.

He went at Sven Larrson's urging to a shabby dance hall in the port area. 'My new friends will be there,' Sven said, running long fingers through his shock of straw-stalky hair. 'The Vikings, eh? We love to dance. Also plunder and pillage, if possible.' He chuckled. 'But you'll be safe with me.'

Sven had wasted no time on arriving in Geraldton: the first evening there, he'd headed for the bar of the waterfront hotel where they were staying and struck up conversation with compatriots working in the fishing industry. 'Most of the boats working out of here have Norwegians or Danes or Swedes as crewmen,' he told Harry. 'Good money in it. And better weather than where we come from.'

In the hall there were three men to every woman. Harry didn't get a dance all evening, but he didn't mind that.

Standing near the door, listening to the piano and fiddle and rowdy voices, whistling along quietly with familiar tunes, or swigging from Sven's whisky flask, he let his thoughts drift. When this series of coastal installation tasks was over, what was he going to do? Did he want to stay with electromagnetic engineering, or might he find some way of learning to pilot a flying machine? There were rapid developments both in wireless and in aircraft. Could the two things come together somehow? Max reckoned that before long it would be possible for aircraft to send and receive wireless signals. Perhaps there'll be an opening for me, thought Harry.

He yawned, feeling a bit giddy now. The fiddle had begun to squawk at him, and his eyes ached. He walked outside, leaned against a fence and took a few deep breaths. This wasn't the place for him. He wanted to be with Nellie, talk with her, put his arm around her shoulder.

Sven appeared beside him, holding out the flask.

'No thanks, Sven. Had enough whisky for one night.'

'Naw, naw, c'mon, young fella,' Sven remonstrated. 'This is no time to knock off. Just starting. Plenty of night ahead. I know somewhere to enjoy ourselves. This way, with me.' He steered Harry along the street and down a smelly lane to a dilapidated weatherboard building. Harry, stumbling behind Sven, found himself in a little parlour where half a dozen Japanese women sat around, nodding at him. Sven spoke to the one who had come to the door, and then turned to Harry.

'Seven and six,' he said.

'Eh?' Harry was finding it hard to concentrate. He stifled another fuddled yawn.

'Seven shillings and sixpence each. Got your share with you?'

Harry frowned, and Sven said impatiently, 'Wake up, mate. What money do you have in your pocket?'

Harry pulled out a handful of coins and stared at them as if trying to remember what they were. Sven took some from him and passed them to the woman in charge. Then he pointed to her two youngest-looking companions. They stood up. Sven chose one of them and went along a passage with her. The other one beckoned to Harry, who followed her drowsily. Leading him into a dingy room, she turned towards him, took one of his hands in hers and placed it on her breast. He didn't move.

'Shy man!' she giggled. 'Shy man!' Stepping back, she lifted her loose shiny purple dress over her head. Underneath it she wore nothing at all. Then she tugged at his belt, drew him down on a thin floor-level mattress, undid his clothing, and rubbed her body rhythmically against his.

As the first fit of shuddering stopped and he flopped back on the mattress, his stomach began to heave and a jet of bile-soured whisky splattered across the floor.

Seven

The war came with its bluster of bugles and posters. Having just gone back to Darwin for maintenance work at the wireless station there, Harry wrote to his parents: 'I'm going to sign up,' he told them, 'with the aim of getting into one of the Royal Flying Corps squadrons.' Just how to do so was unclear to him, but there must surely be some kind of training he could undertake. A few Australians, he'd heard, were already RFC recruits. If this war lasted long, some of it would be fought in the air, he was certain of that; and here was his chance to go aloft into the future.

His hopes tripped at the first enlistment hurdle. He failed the medical examination.

Dismayed, he questioned the examining doctor: 'Are you sure? I haven't been aware of any problem with my eyes. I do a lot of reading and close work.'

'But you're short-sighted. Myopic. It means you can't see distant things clearly. So you won't ever get permission to learn how to pilot an aeroplane.'

Swallowing his chagrin, Harry applied to go overseas as a non-combatant engineer specialising in wireless communication. This too was refused.

'The Government requires you,' said the official letter sternly, 'to contribute to the development of wireless on the home front. It is work that will be vital for Australia's defence. You are to remain at your present address and await instructions.'

Stuck in Darwin with hardly anything to do, Harry soon became fidgety. Scant information came about what was expected of him, so he shrugged and did little else but check and recheck the equipment he had installed a year earlier, keep a record of transmissions, read anything he could find, and think moodily about Nellie. There was a brief flurry of excitement in September over reports of the action in German New Guinea, not far away, where Australian forces in their first engagement of the war took control of the German wireless station at Bitapaka. But once that drama subsided there was nothing much of interest for Harry. Occasional routine messages to and from coastal shipping did nothing to stir the blood or sharpen the brain. All the big action was on the other side of the world. This war could keep him tied up here with petty duties for months, or even longer. Boredom and frustration gnawed at him.

No-one else in this ungainly little town knew anything much about wireless engineering. A few months earlier, with the last couple of north-western coastal stations set up at Wyndham and Roebourne, Sven had headed back down to Perth. A letter told Harry that Max, supervising repairs on the Applecross mast when the war began, was interned with a group of other 'aliens' on Rottnest Island amid fears about German use of wireless for spying. 'Ludicrous!' muttered

Harry as he read the news. Resident in Australia for years, Schank had never shown any strong attachment to the country of his birth. This war was projecting enmity where none existed, erecting barriers between friends. What folly!

Early the next year Harry found himself in naval uniform with the rank of warrant officer – but with unchanged duties. The Naval Board had assumed control of Amalgamated Wireless, and at each coastal service location all station staff willy-nilly became NCOs.

Being billeted at the Hotel Victoria month after month was tolerable at first, but became tedious when the government took over the hotel and closed its public bar.

'Nationalising liquor supplies in the Territory! Why on earth are they doing that?' he asked the frowzy-cheeked barmaid, Mabel, when she told him there would soon be no more drinking on the premises.

'If you wanna believe the official excuse, it's to curb the sly-grog trade up here,' she said, mopping the counter half-heartedly with a limp grey rag. 'But what I hear is they just wanna prevent working-class folk from getting together and talking up trouble. Another thing, too – if they control sales they can raise prices, eh, and scoop up revenue for the Federal budget. Anyway, whatever the reason, they're turning off the taps and so I'm out of a job.'

Harry had never regarded the Victoria as particularly convivial, but at least it used to feel like a hotel. Not any longer. In the evenings there was nothing going on and little to talk about. Men rested their elbows on the rail of the wide verandas, smoking and murmuring.

'It's become nuthin more 'n a run-down boarding house,' grumbled Bob Carver, a grizzled-headed railway foreman who had the room next to Harry's. 'Most of the tucker they dish up for us now is just plain horrible, innit? That grey mushy cabbage – phew! And them carrots always taste of kerosene.'

'You're getting a bit fussy, Bob,' said Harry, straight-faced. Teasing always got a rise out of cantankerous old Carver. 'Next you'll be complaining about delicacies like the bony potatoes or the cardboard strips of meat.'

'No joking matter, mate. The bad food's just a sign of bigger problems. There's plenty for working men to complain about if you stop and think. You oughta drop in on one of our Friday night meetings in the back room downstairs and listen to the union secretary. He can tell you a thing or two about what Gilruth's up to.'

Harry knew that a small group of union men gathered regularly to warm up their grievances against Gilruth, the Territory's severe and unpopular administrator. The next Friday, for want of anything else to do, he sat at the back of their meeting room. The speech-making struck him as tediously bombastic. When it was over he browsed through the books set out on a table and bought a second-hand copy of Bellamy's *Looking Backward*.

He tried reading the novel in bed to while away the muggy evenings, tilting the pages towards the light, and fanning his sweaty face with the *Northern Territory Times* – all it was good for. Flying ants swarmed over the kerosene lamp, singeing their wings, and mosquitoes whined relentlessly around the net that covered his bed.

Set in a glorious utopian future at the end of the twentieth century, *Looking Backward* imagined an 'enfranchisement of humanity' and there was much in this to appeal to Harry. Some of the inventive details spurred him to think of possible ways of enhancing them. Instead of Bellamy's idea of having music relayed into everyone's home through a kind of cable telephone, why couldn't the beautiful sounds of singers and orchestras be transmitted eventually by wireless? But as he closed the book and thought about its evocation of what it called a 'dazzling future' for mankind, he was conscious that the widening conflict in Europe had cast a giant shadow over any hopes of steady progress towards a world united in scientific endeavour and social improvement. Bellamy's vision belonged to a more blithely optimistic era.

That, thought Harry, was partly why union men like Bob Carver were so full of grouches these days. They could surely see, even if they wouldn't admit, that workers and bosses alike were now menaced by something bigger and uglier than class conflict. Something that would not end well.

Harry found it hard now to get a good night's sleep. He kept a flask of whisky on hand, but if he drank much of it the blood would thump and thud and throb its way around his head like an inescapable drumbeat when he lay down, and in the darkness he imagined he could hear battalions of white ants champing their rhythmic way through the walls of his little room.

When he did sleep, there was a recurring nightmare. He would be walking with Nellie through the zoo at night; no-one else could be seen; and then a lion bounded over a wall, seized Nellie in its jaws and carried her off down a bushy path. When he tried to call for help, no sound came from his mouth.

Every day the clock seemed slower. Harry's wireless equipment often stayed silent for hours on end. It hardly took him ten minutes to skim the parochial little newspaper. He'd been given a small desk but apart from routine reports there was nothing much to write except brief letters to his parents. He took up pipe-smoking and it became a lethargic ritual, sucking and puffing idly until the last acrid whiff was gone, then tapping out the dottle, packing in another plug of coarse-cut from the pouch, lighting up again, watching the reeky wisps dissolve. A mild distraction, no more; the tedium was unrelieved. Having to dawdle through the day like this irked him, but what could he turn to? Though the Navy had become his employer, he had little contact with enlisted men or access to significant information about any activities of the armed services. He was avid for reports of Australia's pilots in the Middle East, hearing that wireless contact with aeroplanes had become possible, and wanted to know all the technical details. He wrote to his parents begging for any information they could send from Sydney newspapers about what was now being called radio-telegraphy.

The men who worked alongside him in the little office with the big name, Defence Support Services, were a dull lot, and there seemed to be no congenial company outside it. He yearned to strike up conversation with a woman, almost any woman – had even flirted half-heartedly with Mabel the ill-favoured barmaid before she lost her job. But no-one he'd encountered anywhere in this town could push aside for long his troubled memories of Nellie.

He became more and more mopish. At the end of the stifling afternoons he would sometimes go for a solitary walk around the port area and through Chinatown, along Cavenagh Street from Bennett Street to the Esplanade. The narrow lanes on either side, foul and dark, exuded the smells of offal and excrement, putrid vegetables and stale fish. Behind the street-front shops and stores he glimpsed huddled tenements held together with wooden poles, lumps of stone, flattened kerosene tins, battered scraps of galvanised iron. Easy to see that the government's attempts to relocate 'these Celestials', as the local paper liked to call the Chinese, had been futile. Harry had heard it said that they were comfortable among the cockroaches and beetles and the stench of decay. Unlikely and probably unfair – though you couldn't blame folk, thought Harry, for being anxious about vermin and the spread of diseases – smallpox, malaria, leprosy. Some Chinese men, twenty or more he'd been told, were confined to an isolation camp at Leper Point, a rough sandy beach across the harbour, halfway to Channel Island.

⸺

One morning he woke, could see nothing, and thought for a terrifying instant he had gone blind overnight – until his sudden movement dislodged the huge batlike moth that had somehow got under the netting and settled on the bridge of his nose, spreading its wings over his eyes. In the ensuing weeks, that hideous sensation often came back when sleep approached or receded, blocking his sight and enshrouding him in dread, as if the future he had so ardently imagined would be forever lost to view.

'I'll have to snap out this mood somehow,' he told himself irritably. 'I need to be doing something. Use my brain.' He decided to write down miscellaneous observations to help while away the idle hours at the office. So he acquired an exercise book and began to make diary jottings on whatever crossed his mind.

On the first page he pencilled a few thoughts about what he had seen in the dirty alleys of Chinatown, and that prompted a further reflection:

It reminds me of the time, back in South Perth, when Nellie and I were out for a walk with young Doris and a couple of coolies came jogging along the track. I remember Doris recoiled as if they were hardly human. Although I don't share that kind of revulsion, I wonder what place there will be for such people in the future. A world of new things, new ways, a world shaped and mastered by science, a world of wireless communication and aeroplanes – how could the Chinese belong there? If the 'enfranchisement of humanity' imagined in Bellamy's story ever comes to pass, will they have any part in it? Or those Japanese and Malays I saw in Broome? We all want the march of progress to resume when this war is over, but can it really overcome all isolation, all separation, taking every race and nation forward into prosperity together? I don't see it happening.

The next day, after reading news from Gallipoli and brooding about his exclusion from active service, he wrote:

When our troops come back after the war, I suppose a lot of them are going to be permanently marked – for better or worse – by what they're doing and seeing over there. But those of us who haven't had that experience will be marked too. It's likely I'll always feel I've missed out on something important.

In a later entry he tried to explain to himself how his thoughts about Nellie these days were changing.

It's been over three years. During that time her phantom has never left me for long, but lately my remembering has begun to take on a different shape. For a while after she vanished, thinking of her used to feel like drawing up details from a deep well and inspecting them for possible clues. Now it's something else: I feel more like someone kneeling at a graveside.

It was an even muggier evening than usual, and his clouds of pipe-smoke were no deterrent to the mosquitoes, but Harry lingered on the hotel veranda in the twilight, re-reading Freddie Dingle's letter. This wasn't the first time Freddie had written to him. His news of Max Schank's incarceration as an alien, and odds and ends about others who had worked with them on the Applecross station, arrived not long after the outbreak of war. There had been a further letter a few months later about nothing in particular but it smelt of dank despondency.

…A couple of my close mates have left on a troopship, and I don't know what to do with myself. Too old, too fat. The army's too bloody fastidious to want me. My wife has gone off to stay with her folks in Guildford. I'm on my own in South Perth, hoping to pick up more regular work. Not much of it around, though…

And now came this third letter, with its horrible news.

…Young Doris Biddle went missing, and a couple of days later they found her body washed up on the shore near Como

jetty. She'd been strangled: her belt was still wound tight
around her neck...

It sent a spasm of pity through Harry's guts as he pictured
the violent assault, the life being choked out of her, the river
plucking at her girlish freckles and bloating her flesh. And it
stirred up a tormenting fear about Nellie's fate.

But that wasn't all. Freddie's letter went on to recount a
gruesome sequel to Doris's murder. Suspicion had soon fallen
on an elderly man, known around South Perth for years but
ostracised since the war began because people thought he was
some sort of German.

You'll remember him well, Harry – old Fritz. Turns out
he wasn't a Hun after all, seems he may actually have
been Hungarian, or something like that, though not much
difference I suppose. Well, someone had seen old Fritz talking
with Doris over his front fence not long before she disappeared,
offering her lollies, a bit too friendly. No evidence of anything
else. But boys started throwing stones at his windows and
people muttered at him or avoided him. Then yesterday
morning Fritz's body was found propped against the zoo gates.
On his jacket sleeve someone had pinned a piece of paper, and
the block lettering read A DIRTY BEAST. The side of his
skull had been staved in with a brick.

Putting the letter aside, Harry recalled brief conversations
with Fritz during his own days in South Perth. The man was
often at his gate when Harry walked down to the jetty in the
mornings, and they would exchange greetings. It was hard to
believe that Fritz could have killed Doris: harmless, tubby old

coot, looked a bit odd with his wide flat face and protruding lower lip that a parakeet could almost have perched on, but amiable enough – and so lame and wheezy, anyway, that he just wouldn't have been capable of killing her and disposing of the corpse.

The next day Harry took out his exercise book and wrote:

The savage way people turned on that old man – it sickens me. People need scapegoats, and these days foreignness is tantamount to guilt. There's poor bloody Max marooned on Rottnest. And around here some people shun the Chinese as if they weren't human. The world seems to be regressing crazily into a habit of hating. Will this disappear again when the war ends, or is it going to persist?

A fear of foreigners. A habit of hating. And of all the hostilities erupting in Australia, he thought, none could be more perverted and pathetic in its patriotism than the ice-cream cart battle. His mother had forwarded a letter written by her sister Muriel in Broken Hill.

It happened on New Year's Day. A train full of hundreds of holiday picnickers in open wagons set out from our Railway Town terminal in the morning. Before the train left, an ice-cream cart pulled by an old nag had driven slowly past and picnickers waved to the two turbaned men aboard it. The cart was well known around Broken Hill, you see, but on this day it carried a flag – which no-one on the train recognised as Turkish. Later, when the train drew near to its picnic destination, the ice-cream cart was seen close to the line, and the two Mohammedans were crouching beside it with rifles.

They fired repeatedly at close range as the wagons of defenceless picnickers went past. After killing four and wounding several others, they retreated and took cover some distance off. Armed pursuers eventually shot them.

Well, you can imagine the fury at what these Turks had done. Gangs turned against other aliens, burning the German Club to the ground and storming the Afghan camel-drivers' camp. But if you ask me, the local folk have to take some of the blame. Many people in Broken Hill had been ridiculing Moslem customs, and these two foolish unhappy men apparently wanted to avenge the insults. What a horrible comedy! What a shameful tragedy!

But there was a realm of truly noble action elsewhere – Harry still believed that. To his parents he sent money and a request. Many weeks later a heavy parcel arrived: Douglas Mawson's *The Home of the Blizzard: Being the Story of the Australasian Antarctic Expedition*. Evening after evening Harry pored over the two solid volumes, and after reaching the end he re-read large sections. Although he thought Mawson's prose was mostly pedestrian, the exploits thrilled him. Here was heroism, here was prowess, here was the extreme edge of human effort, and darkness looming beyond the edge. It was only a couple of years ago that newspapers had carried the shocking news from Antarctica: Scott's party had perished while returning from the South Pole, and Mawson's group had also come to grief – Mawson himself surviving by the skin of his teeth but two of his companions dying.

To be sure, Freddie Dingle had made a fair point that day at the Applecross station when he recounted the story of Richardson's epic bike ride around Australia: you didn't have to go to the Antarctic to find heroic endeavour. Pedalling across vast expanses of desert without any companions, that was pretty impressive too, no doubt about it. Yet Mawson's astonishing tale, told in stolid words that carried a simple strength, was about more than individual achievement. Yes, this and that person certainly did accomplish remarkable feats of solo endurance, ingenuity, valour; but beyond the personal qualities of Mawson and other expedition members, they all worked together as companions in extreme circumstances, gave each other hard-bitten support, their roles interlocking so that they functioned as a kind of family in which even the sled dogs had a companionable place. Only as a desperate last resort, nearly starving after most of his supplies disappeared into a crevasse, did Mawson kill any of these animals for food – unlike that cold bugger Amundsen, who relied on the slaughter of dogs as part of his plans for provisioning.

Harry turned back from the main narrative to the heightened rhetoric of the foreword by Mawson's colleague and editor McLean, a tribute that evoked the spirit of exploration as transcending nationality and converging with scientific endeavour. It began with a lofty epigraph from the poet Browning, and he re-read the passage slowly until he could recite it to himself. Into a few lines it seemed to bring together the sombre and the blithe, compressing them in a way that spoke to him personally with a strange resonance:

> *Nor on thee yet*
> *Shall burst the future, as successive zones*
> *Of several wonder open on some spirit*
> *Flying secure and glad from heaven to heaven.*

What poem it came from, and what real or imaginary person the prophecy addressed, Harry didn't know; but as he drew the words into himself he felt his mood lift buoyantly. They revived something of the ardent, expectant faith he'd tried to express to Nellie on that afternoon in South Perth the first time they'd walked out together: faith in what lay ahead for mankind, a future bursting with zones of wonder and flights of the spirit. The old trance came over him again, a familiar yet half-forgotten sensation of undulating through the air as if at one with its secret currents.

But rustling faintly within the whoosh of exhilaration there was still something else, just perceptible, like a wishful, wistful sigh.

Part 2

1932 – 1933

Eight

The small piece of broken mirror, propped in a cleft of a paperbark tree, reflected a face creased with disappointment. Only one of his eyes registered that reflection; the other was opaque and sightless, with scarring around its socket. But he could see all too clearly how his life had changed in the twenty years since his departure from Sydney.

With no job to go to now, and no companion to care whether he looked presentable, the daily removal of stubble from chin and cheeks hardly felt worthwhile. Shaving was a routine that helped to fill in empty time at the start of the day. It was also a way of trying to retain some sense of normality and self-respect. It showed he hadn't let himself go, wasn't hopelessly down in the dumps.

And today, anyway, there was someone he was planning to meet again after a long gap.

A few cups of strong tea would set him up for the morning with the help of an oatmeal cake wangled from the family in the tent next to his, the Sewells. They had set up a small griddle behind their tent, protected from the wind by hessian sacks that the zoo had donated to the camp, and Mrs Sewell would cook an extra piece for him when she could. It wasn't all one-sided. He would share with the Sewells whatever he caught in the river. Standing calf-deep in the shallows for an hour or more at a time, trousers rolled up, twine held between thumb and forefinger, he did his best to entice black bream or flathead to take an interest in the sacrificial worms impaled on wire hooks at the far end of the twine. Success was infrequent.

But now he just needed water for boiling. Billycan in hand, he made his way from the little encampment down to the sandy waterside. On this side of the bridge the Canning flowed strongly towards its junction with the Swan. As he crouched to fill the billy, he squeezed stale air between his teeth in a tuneless wheezy hiss, substitute for the melodic whistling of jauntier days. The river was whispering something back that he couldn't catch.

He hadn't seen Freddie Dingle for nearly twenty years, and there'd been no contact since that exchange of letters while Harry was in Darwin during the war. It was just by chance, a few days ago, that he'd overheard Freddie's name mentioned by one of the other blokes camped here by the Canning River, old Jim Kirby, who told him Freddie was back in South Perth.

'He'd been battling for a while, Freddie had, even before the slump came along,' said Jim. 'Had a crook spin. Moved with his family to Bridgetown at one stage – this'd be just before you came back from your time up north – and he tried to make a go of it labouring on some bloke's farm, but it didn't work out. We lost touch for a while. I've heard his wife has left him – not for the first time. Anyhow, now he's here in South Perth again, but on a relief gang, not easy at his age, poor bugger – must be pushing sixty. Dozens of them have spent months shovelling and barrowing sand to modify the golf course opposite the zoo there. Artificial gullies and hillocks. In the middle of a bloody depression, and what does the government tell workingmen they must do for a pittance when there's no real work around? Rebuild a playground for silvertails!'

With nothing else to do, Harry set out early. There would be plenty of time to fill in at the other end; finding the group of relief workers might not take long but Freddie probably couldn't slip away for a chinwag until later in the day. That was all right by Harry. He'd wander around some of the familiar streets, and perhaps while away an hour or two down at the Point, have a gander at the old derelict mill and the nearby pool he'd once walked around with Nellie.

After that he'd look for Freddie, and see whether they could arrange to meet towards the end of the afternoon, probably at the old Windsor Hotel on the corner of Mends Street and Suburban Road.

Harry didn't do much drinking these days – seldom had any coins in his pocket anyway – but sometimes the need for company had taken him into a pub for a beer or two. Just exchanging a few words, even with a stranger, could make him feel less like a bit of driftwood. There'd been some odd encounters, too, and he recalled one of them as he set out on his walk towards South Perth. A garrulous Kiwi, newly arrived in Perth, had buttonholed Harry and talked on and on about having been in Napier a few months back when the big earthquake hit the town and killed hundreds.

Swigging from a bottle of Emu, he spoke of the disaster in a loud, agitated way that made it seem like an image of all the turmoil that society was going through – 'Everything we thought was solid just collapsed,' Harry remembered him saying with a fleck of spittle on his cheek. 'Before we knew what was happening, the brick walls of big buildings just rippled and groaned. Burst open like gushing fountains.'

Picking his way now along the Como shore, Harry counted himself lucky that the overnight drizzle had gone and the usual winter wind had dropped; the morning was becalmed. But bleakness held everything in its grip. Scum-smeared blowfish flotsam marked the high-tide line. When he reached the jetty he stood for a while, remembering young Doris Biddle and imagining the dispassionate slap of water against her lifeless limbs. Then he turned away from the river and followed a shell-strewn track that meandered through low scrub, gradually rising past a scatter of houses until it took him to a spot he knew. It was where he and Nellie had paused with Doris on their walk twenty years before. That had been a day of seemingly simple happiness. Now the smell of soot from Como chimneys hung damply under a scowling sky.

⤳

'Geez, what happened to your eye?'

Harry looked down and finished rolling his cigarette. 'Stupid bloody accident.' He ran the tip of his tongue along the paper and tidied up the ends before adding: 'Came off my pushbike, swerving to avoid a yappy dog. Front wheel got caught in the gutter, bike fell on top of me, and the end of the handlebar went into my eye.'

Shaking his head at the perversity of misfortune, Freddie took a long swallow from his glass. 'Too damned noisy in here,' he said, wiping the froth from his lips as he nodded towards the door. Beer in hand, they went out and sat side by side on the footpath, backs to the wall.

Freddie had the rank smell of mangy dog, and his breath was sour. He was almost unrecognisably different from the man Harry had last seen just before leaving for Geraldton so long ago. Being unemployed for several years had knocked the stuffing out of him. He looked weary and defeated, had lost weight, lost his chuckle, lost his wife and children too. 'Haven't seen or heard from them in months. They all went off to stay with her ladyship's parents when I got sent to the camp at Blackboy Hill last year.'

'Eh? What camp's that?'

'An old army site, about a dozen miles from here up in the hills, along the York Road near the national park. More than a thousand of us were put up there, unemployed men, and they loved ordering us around, do this, don't do that – bloody strict! The way they ran the camp you'd think we were prisoners of war. But we kept meek as mice, and did the maintenance jobs we were told to do, damned drudgery, because it brought us five bob a week and that was a hell of a lot better than nothing. Well, after a year they moved most of us out of Blackboy Hill and put us on other relief schemes, so now I'm back here in South Perth, as you know, with a gang of no-hopers just like me, all doing barrow and shovel work on the golf links. Boring as a vicar's tea party. Anyway, tell me what you've been up to. Looks as if you're down on your luck too, mate.'

'No regular work since my accident – early last year, that was.' Harry sucked in a long breath and blew smoke from his nostrils before going on. 'For a couple of months over the summer I was doing deliveries for the Chinese gardeners. I'd got to know one of them, Ah Sing, and when he broke his leg he asked me to take his vegetable cart around the streets until he got better. He trusted me to take the money to him at the end of each day. And I collected manure, too, for his garden: there was a little shovel at the side of the cart, and a hessian bag, and none of the horseshit was to be left on the road. I liked the vegetable round. Hardly any payment, but I could take a bit of food away at the end of the run – cabbages, mainly, under each arm – and exchange some of it with neighbours for soup bones or bread and cheese. It kept the wolf from the door.'

'A lot different, though, from what you had in mind when you first came to Perth all those years ago.'

'Too right. I had plans back then, big dreams...' Harry lifted his eyebrows and dropped the corners of his mouth ruefully in a kind of facial shrug. 'Things just didn't turn out well. After Nellie disappeared my luck evaporated too.'

'You've never heard anything about her?'

'Nothing.' Stubbing out the cigarette, he picked up his glass and inspected the froth line.

His memories of Nellie – little incidents and images, things seen and said and felt – were stored now in an orderly array on a shelf of his mind, like jars of fruit preserves shut away in a cupboard in his mother's Collaroy kitchen.

'Been any other women in your life?' Freddie probed.

Harry shook his head. The sudden loss of Nellie, the long bewilderment that followed, the accumulated weight of yearning and grief – all this had lain athwart the flow of feelings for so many years that he had never been able to form a happy attachment to anyone else. Whatever it was that had kept Nellie mysteriously remote from him – indifference, fear, death, something unimaginable – seemed also to have distanced him from the possibility of companionship with others. Part of his life had been severed. It was like the amputation of a limb.

But lust could often grip him suddenly: catching sight of Mavis Sewell breastfeeding her youngest when he walked past their tent, or happening to glance at the well-turned ankle of some woman crossing the street – he felt an ache in the pit of his stomach, and when he lay down alone at night the images would come back to him and swell into lurid fantasies.

He wanted to tell Freddie more about the vacant years, but stopped himself. No point in sharing his misery. They drank in silence for a while. Unvoiced memories slid around in his head. He could have talked about all that wasted time in Darwin during the war. About the frustration of being marooned there with so little to do while other men were seeing action overseas. About having to relinquish all hope of flying, reduced to following enviously the newspaper reports of aviators' exploits. About failing to get advancement in the world of wireless, expecting to find something better but missing out on the few chances that came his way. About sinking gradually into a state of mind that bordered on the morose as he felt, year by year, the long slow diminishment of his exuberant youthful ambitions.

Only a few bright spots had kept him going. He was temporarily buoyed by Smithy's arrival in Maylands in August 1928 at the end of the first non-stop trans-Australian flight. That year had been an illustrious one for Australian aviation, with Smithy flying all the way across the Pacific and Wilkins crossing the Arctic Ocean and then charting a large stretch of Antarctic land from the air. The magic of powered flight: once Harry had imagined that he himself would become one of the bold spirits leading the way adventurously into an expansive future. Instead, he'd become an odd-jobber with a bung eye.

As best he could, he had kept himself informed about developments in wireless technology, clipping articles from the newspaper. In 1927 a short-wave beam system made direct communication possible between Australia and England. Applecross became a feeder station for international radio-grams, weather forecasts, news bulletins. And just this year a commercial station, 6PR, began broadcasting from the Applecross site.

But such things might as well have been happening on another planet as far as most of the local families were concerned. Hardly anyone he knew had a wireless set in the home. There was no work at all to be had around South Perth now. Men walked the streets without purpose or sat listlessly on verandas. Drab women hung dusty rugs over their clotheslines and whacked every mote out of them in a rhythm of throbbing bafflement.

'So where are you living now?' Freddie asked him, interrupting the reverie.

'On the bloody edge, to tell the truth. For the last couple of months I've been in a tent, down past Canning Bridge there. Couldn't scrape together enough rent money any more.'

Clicking his tongue sympathetically, Freddie reached for Harry's empty glass. 'Want a refill?'

'I'm skint.'

'It's OK mate, I can shout you one.'

'Thanks, all right, yes.'

When Freddie came back outside with a pint in each hand, they began to talk about people they remembered from before the war: men they had worked with on the wireless station, and neighbours from those days in South Perth.

'Kept in touch with Sven?' Harry asked.

Freddie shook his head. 'Died about ten years back. You know what he used to be like – well, the grog made him more and more peevish, snaky, always looking for trouble. Silly galoot got such a skinful one time that he picked a fight with a dirty big ox of a man who knocked him flat with one punch. Busted his neck when he fell, bang, and that was that.'

'Poor fool. And Max Schank? You wrote to me early in the war, remember, saying he'd been interned on Rottnest. So what happened to him after that, do you know?'

'Well I can tell you this much, they only kept the aliens over on the island for a year before they moved them all to some godforsaken place in New South Wales, out beyond Liverpool I think it was. Sort of barracks. Thousands of them cooped up there like animals right till the end of the war, was what I heard. Then shipped off to Germany.'

'He didn't deserve any of that. A good man. Remember how proud he was when the aerial went up?' Harry took a swig. 'He used to make us laugh, too, didn't he, with his mixed-up words. If he didn't agree with something, it was either a "mute point" or a "bane of contention", eh?' They grinned at each other. 'But a decent bloke, anyway.'

'What about the folks we used to know around here?' Harry went on. 'I heard old Polly Milligan dropped dead in the street, years ago. And Jim Kirby told me the boarding house closed down after Mrs Riven took ill. What news of the Biddles?'

Freddie stared into his glass for a while before responding. There was a look on his face that Harry hadn't seen before and couldn't interpret.

'Poor buggers,' Freddie said, wiping his mouth and shaking his head. 'Marge got a cancer not long after their girl was killed. Took her off real quick. And Cec just went to pieces: gave up work, moped around, poisoned his liver with heavy drinking. He didn't last long.'

'Must have been terrible to lose young Doris the way they did. She was a sweet kid. Having that happen to your only daughter would be enough to send any parent into the grave.'

Freddie nodded slowly, head down. His cheeks were damp. He blew his nose noisily, started to speak but couldn't shape any words. Putting a hand on the older man's shoulder, Harry could feel the tremor of a suppressed sob. There was more to Freddie, he had always thought, than showed on the surface; but until now he hadn't glimpsed such deep feeling.

After a long silence they took their glasses back inside. 'No thanks,' said Harry in response to a questioning gesture. 'That'll do me.'

As they were starting to turn away from the bar, Harry saw that a man who stood near him had no arms, just stumps that stopped short of where elbows should be. To drink he leant right forward, hunching his shoulders around the glass, gripping it with stumps and mouth, tipping it up clumsily. His nose was round and red as a tomato, and there was a stipple of carbuncular patches on his cheeks, as if he had splashed himself with paint. Seeing that he was watched, he called for a refill and turned to Harry with a jerk of his jaw and a crackle of phlegm. 'Hey, shiner! Get the money for this from my pocket, will you?' Harry had to stand very close to him. The man's skin was grimy. So was his pocket, and there was no money in it. 'Deeper,' he growled, chest rattling. 'Deeper!'

Nine

Trudging back towards the Canning Bridge camp as the last warmth leaked from the afternoon, he told himself he should have talked more to Freddie about the disconsolate years of searching fruitlessly for Nellie. It would probably have been a relief, he thought, if I'd opened up and told him how utterly miserable it's been all this while.

When the war finished he hadn't been able to decide what to do with himself. There was no decent work going in Darwin. AWL had nothing more for him – thank you, well done, goodbye and good luck. Government officials shook their heads, too: all the departments up there were over-staffed. So he drifted down to Perth, picking up work only fitfully over the next year. With so many soldiers returning, there wasn't enough solid employment to go around. His engineering credentials and testimonial letters attracted no interest. There would surely be more opportunities in Sydney, and he wanted to see his parents again, but going back east would be impossible until he had saved enough for the boat trip – hard to do unless he could get better-paid employment. So he lingered, and the months slipped by.

Throughout this dreary period, thoughts of finding Nellie had preoccupied him. He'd renewed his enquiries to the police. Tom Torrence, it turned out, had left for a job somewhere in the goldfields. The lethargic new constable at the South Perth station shook his head uncomprehendingly when Harry asked about the Weston case, and then kept him waiting while he muttered away to himself about procedure as he searched the grubby shelves of a cupboard behind his desk.

'Nope,' he declared eventually. 'No information has come to hand since 1912. This last entry here says, *The matter remains unsolved but is now closed.*'

Yet Harry would not let it close. He'd gone next to visit old Mrs Milligan, just across the street from the former bakery. Conversation proved to be difficult: in the few years since his last contact with her, Polly Milligan had become so deaf he could hardly make himself understood. Besides, her mind seemed to be meandering, and he could see that she was vaguely aware of this: she paused in the middle of inconsequential divagations, pudgy finger pressed against her forehead, to murmur, 'Oh botheration! Now I'm getting muddled again.' After half an hour's chatter it was plain enough to Harry that she had heard nothing about the Westons since their disappearance. But she did suggest a line of investigation that hadn't occurred to him. 'Well, there's the church they used to go to,' she said. 'You could try asking there. I s'pose they might know something by now.'

Of course! He should have thought of that. So he went at once to the pastor of the local Methodist church where the

Westons had worshipped regularly. But Rev. George Brindle, being a recent arrival in South Perth, knew nothing of the family. He wore a baggy grey cardigan and a matching face that drooped under the weight of his earnest manner as he listened, all sympathetic nods and frowns, to Harry's tale of a lost love.

'If you'd like to call in again tomorrow, I'll give you an address list of some of my colleagues in the ministry,' he offered. 'Men who are spreading the gospel in other parts of the state. You could write to them with an enquiry. Perhaps someone will have something to tell you about the family's whereabouts. But meanwhile' – Brindle leant forward, hands clasped beneath his chin to show sincerity – 'the good Lord can help you as you struggle with your lonely isolation. At a time of trouble like this, you need the family of Christian brethren and sisters to surround you and sustain you with faith and hope and charity. Our congregation would like to extend the hand of fellowship to you in your hour of need.' He beamed with unctuous goodwill.

'Righto,' said Harry, looking away, 'thanks very much. But it's not really my cup of tea. I can manage pretty well on my own, really.'

The truth, he admitted reluctantly to himself as he left the manse, was that he had no clear idea of how to 'manage'. His life was drifting. He felt acutely alone, and although the blandishments of religion held no appeal he did yearn for company. But the problem was that the companionship he wanted was with a particular woman, long since gone from his life.

A few evenings later, as he sat down to write the batch of letters to more than a dozen Methodist ministers, he took something from between the pages of a book. With thumb and fingertip he held her cherished image. Of the three photographs he had taken of Nellie at the zoo, this was the one he would gaze at most often, most fondly. In the other two her face was indistinct, half turned away as she watched an elephant with one of its front feet lifted and its trunk an inverted question mark. But in the picture he now tilted towards the flickering candlelight, Nellie faced the camera with that dimple-framed smile he remembered so well. Her teeth were as white as her muslin dress, and sunlight shone in the waves of her hair. Behind her, and across her shoulder, was a large splodge of shadow.

If only he had used his pocket Brownie more often that day, and in the weeks that followed! Just a handful of snapshots, in all. Most of them had come out well enough. But then, trying to steady the little camera against the boat's rail one windy afternoon, he had lost his balance and in an instant it slipped from his hand into the unforgiving water. No chance of retrieval.

Whenever he gazed at her image she would re-emerge for a moment from the past, from her unknown hiding place. Still, she remained partly in shadow. Looking at the photograph again now, it occurred to him for the first time that in some ways Nellie and he weren't really learning as much about each other back then as they thought they were. It was all preliminary, without much insight. Perhaps, he thought, that's because I hadn't yet got to know myself very well and the same was probably true for her, though neither of us recognised at the time how slowly any self-knowledge develops.

In the letters, he gave the South Perth post office as his address. Replies trickled back during the next few weeks, all of them politely brief and devoid of useful information.

But at that time the postal service had brought him one letter with grave news from his mother, telling of his father's sudden death.

…It was a heart attack, quite unexpected, poor man. He'd been chopping wood in the backyard. I was nearby, hanging a load of clothes on the line. I heard him cry out, and turned to see him topple forward across the chopping block, axe still gripped in his hand. It took me just a few seconds to reach him but already he was as dead as the axe. A terrible shock for me, but for him I suppose it was good to go quickly. Bert wouldn't have wanted to endure drawn-out suffering, would he?

I'll go ahead with the funeral and burial arrangements. I know you won't be able to afford to travel to Sydney on the new transcontinental railway – people say it's expensive and unreliable – and the sea route wouldn't get you here in good time.

Bert was a lovely husband to me, and you can be sure he was enormously proud of you, son.

That was more than a decade ago, and his mother's death had come a few years later. Now, back in his little makeshift tent at the Canning Bridge camp, he thought of the stories his father had told him each evening when he was a small child – a chain of amusing and reassuring tales in which assorted animals would find themselves in the very situations that Harry was experiencing at the time: making friends, learning to read, falling off the fence and spraining a wrist, starting school, or deciding what to do with a smelly dead fish found on the beach. If animals could surmount such challenges, surely he could do so himself. In later years his mother's dinner-table readings from Dickens brought him richer food.

There were not many books in the family home, but three that had pride of place were *The King's English*, *Pears' Shilling Cyclopaedia* and *Chambers's Dictionary*. Bert Hopewell consulted the Fowler brothers on distinguishing properly between shall and will, may and might, and other essential items of linguistic knowledge. He checked the cyclopaedia frequently on synonyms and antonyms, correct abbreviations, medical terms and much else. But the lexical riches compiled by Chambers were his special delight. Whenever an unfamiliar word came up or any doubt hovered over some nuance of meaning, there would be an enthusiastic exclamation: 'Let's look it up, lad!' This seemed to happen often at the dinner table, and Harry could picture his dad laying down knife and fork, pushing back his chair, fetching the big book, and turning its pages reverently, as if handling sacred scripture. Then he would run a stubby finger down the columns.

'Kindly...Kingdom...Kinsman...Kiss...Kitchen...here it is now, Kith: "The persons whom one knows, considered collectively; one's friends and neighbours; as in the phrase *kith and kin*, acquaintances and relatives." The derivation links it to the word *known*. Got that, Harry?'

His mother had been nearly ten years younger than her husband, and it occurred now to Harry that he had never had much insight into the relationship between his parents. It always seemed comfortable and calm but anything further was unclear. While he had never witnessed any sign of conflict, Lucy and Bert didn't seem to have much in common. In fact there was a lot he didn't know: how they had come together, how they spent their time before his arrival on the scene, why they chose Collaroy. Lucy was from Broken Hill, Bert grew up in Newtown, he was aware of that; so how had they met, and what had brought them to the northern beaches?

Too late to ask. And some things about any couple's life together were, he supposed, beyond enquiry anyway. What it was like to be inside the closed sphere of a settled twosome he could hardly imagine. Quite opaque to an onlooker. Involuntarily his fingertips moved to touch his damaged eye socket.

What he could be sure about was that his parents were unassuming and kindly – people 'of good character', as the saying went. Had he inherited any of their virtues? They'd had no chattels to leave for him – the little rented house in Collaroy was sparsely furnished – and their demise brought him no material benefit, but he did hope that something of their simple decency had been handed on to him.

Perhaps not. It occurred to him that there was a question mark against his own character. Why had he become unable to surmount the adversity that had dogged him for years? Was he weak? Could he put it all down to misfortune? What had happened to the self-confidence that once seemed to be lifting him bravely into an airborne future?

Ten

Past midday, and the crowd kept growing. Men stood in clumps and exchanged a few words, or milled about, not going anywhere in particular. But although they lingered in Barrack Street, it wasn't like loitering. There was an almost palpable sense of purpose, a spirit of moving along together. On the tip of a tidal swell as it flowed upriver, slowly but strongly: that's how Harry imagined the impetus. Shoulder to shoulder with so many others, he felt something akin to good cheer for the first time in years. Desultory snatches of song lifted their collective mood. Behind him, to the tune of *Daisy Daisy*, someone with a voice like a rasp scraping over tin began rehearsing a sardonic appeal to the Premier they wanted to confront:

> *Mitchell, Mitchell, give us your answer, do!*
> *We're half starving, all because of you.*
> *We shouldn't have to forage,*
> *We can't exist on porridge,*

So get us a job
Worth twenty-five bob
Every week – or good riddance to you!

Claps and guffaws. The crowd outside the Treasury Building had an unbuttoned attitude. Most of the men were jacketless. Several wore frayed shirts, or boots that held the soles and uppers together with twine. A few were unshaven. The smell of stale sweat suggested it was a long while since some of them last had a bath. But it struck Harry suddenly that there was hardly a man among them with an uncovered head. Whether trilby, soft cap, or battered bowler, this was their emblem of residual respectability. He straightened his own hat's brim, and lifted his chin.

'But what's the purpose, exactly?' Harry had asked that morning when Jim Kirby urged him to join the demonstration.

'To stand up and be counted, mate. It's going to be a display of solidarity – that's the point.'

So Harry didn't know quite what to expect, but just being part of this spontaneous assembly of the unemployed was enough for the moment. By now he reckoned the numbers had swollen to at least a couple of thousand, with more still arriving from all directions. The sheer multitude of them would surely make a statement that the government couldn't ignore. Everyone waited.

'Good turnout, eh?' said the man standing next to him, a tall stooping fellow with wispy hair and a sallow colour. Harry nodded. They coughed in shy unison.

'You live in the city?' the stooper asked him.

Harry hesitated. 'South Perth. Well, until a few months ago. Now I'm down near Canning Bridge for the time being.'

'Haven't been southside for years, but me dad used to take us over to the zoo when I was a kid.'

'You'd hardly recognise some of it,' said Harry. 'The foreshore's getting reclaimed, with dredges dumping river mud in the area between Mill Point and the jetty. The Point itself is still bush-covered, mostly, but developers opened up land behind Suburban Road. That was happening fast by the end of the 'twenties. Gone a bit quiet now, of course. The trams have made a difference, too – been operating for ten years across the Causeway, down to Como, and right along Labouchere Road to the zoo entrance.'

'Zoo still the same, I s'pose?'

'No, it's got run down, looks shabby. Only half the number of people working there now that there used to be and some of the exhibits have fallen into disrepair. I heard the Major – *Colonel* Le Souef, I should say, that's what he is these days – wants the State Gardens Board to take charge of it. Anyhow, what about you? Where's home?'

'Subiaco, used to be. Since I lost me job, though, I been way down on the south coast. Might as well've been in prison. We're on strike now. There's about 400 of us came up on the Albany train, with a blunt message for the bloody government.'

Harry nodded. 'I heard about it.'

'Well, I s'pose you know we've been clearing timber around the Frankland River settlement – someone's bright idea for a relief scheme that'd get us away from Perth – outa sight outa mind, but conditions are vile down there, really vile, wet and cold, can't keep warm at night, the food's miserable too, and if you get sick there's no doctor within cooee. All that's bad enough but now the big galoots who run the scheme are trying to put us on a new piecework arrangement – means we can't get a fair price for our yakka, so we downed tools and marched all the way to the Albany station and here we are.'

'Will you go back south if they agree to lift the piecework rate?'

'I'd like to say no. It's a filthy scheme, and no matter how much sugar you put in you can't make strawberry jam out of pigshit. But what choice is there, eh? I had a look around yesterday at the store where I used to have a job: nothing doing. It's as if I'd never worked there. Gives you a sick feeling to see how soon your absence just closes up. Like withdrawing your fist from a bucket of water: it doesn't leave a hole for long.'

There was a commotion at the front of the crowd. A small group had begun to make its way up the Treasury Building steps but was stopped by police. One of the officers had a loudspeaker.

'This gathering is unlawful,' he bellowed, adding sternly as a chorus of boos subsided, 'You're all impeding traffic and causing a public nuisance. There's no point in loitering here.'

'We've got a bone to pick with the Premier!' shouted someone in the middle of the crowd, and there was a rumble of support on all sides.

'The Premier is not available today.' More booing. A thin voice at the back tried to start up with 'Mitchell, Mitchell, give us your answer, do', but trailed away as noise and raucous cries flared up all around them. Mounted troopers came clopping up the street and the crowd began to shuffle and shrink back. No-one seemed to know what to do next; there was no acknowledged leader, and apparently no plan.

Just as the resolute mood had faded into muttering, an upstairs window at the Royal Arcade corner was flung open and a quartet of irreverent demagogues began to shout strident exhortations to those below. Sweating constables struggled through the throng, but as they rushed up the arcade stairs with handcuffs at the ready, an equally vehement voice from a parapet across the street echoed the rhetoric. Heads swivelled, laughter broke out, people clapped. A couple of minutes later, cheering erupted from around the corner in Hay Street, and the crowd surged in that direction. From the balconies of the Theatre Royal and Hotel Metropole other speakers were now holding forth with insolent vigour, to the delight of those on the footpath opposite. The demonstration had turned into a circus, and the police into flustered clowns.

It felt good while it lasted. Harry found himself grinning at strangers. But nothing much had been accomplished, he saw that. No chance of putting their views to the politicians, let alone extracting promises of change. After a while men began to drift away. 'Let's go down to the Esplanade,' someone yelled, 'and work out a plan of action.' Some moved off in that direction, but Harry couldn't see any point in reconvening. He stood in a shoe-shop doorway and rolled a cigarette.

'Goldilocks! Hey, Harry Hopewell!' He looked up. It was Freddie Dingle, crossing the street towards him, a young woman at his side. For a moment Harry thought there was something familiar about her, but no – he didn't know who she was. As they approached, he touched the brim of his hat. Freddie introduced her: Miss Ruth Grace. Short, auburn-haired, very youthful, she had a notebook and pencil in her hand and a pert look on her face. 'She's a reporter, sort of,' said Freddie.

'Would like to be,' she added. 'But there's no place for a woman journalist in a newspaper office. Not in Perth, anyway. Not unless you're happy just to write trivial pieces, social notes.'

'But it seems you've been taking notes here today,' Harry observed, raising an enquiring eyebrow. 'Not many women in the crowd – very bold of you to come along.' And hardly old enough to be called a woman, he thought. Eighteen or nineteen, perhaps, but self-possessed nevertheless.

'Oh, I can look after myself,' she said firmly, with a toss of her head. 'And, yes, I've been jotting down some impressions, things I've seen and heard in the last hour or two. Not for a newspaper, though. I'm writing a report for a wireless broadcast. Do you listen to 6PR?'

Harry shook his head. 'Can't afford a wireless set. But I do know about 6PR: it's broadcasting from the Applecross station, which Freddie and I helped to set up twenty years ago. Long before public radio started, of course.'

Freddie nodded. 'That's just what I was starting to tell Miss Grace. She'd been asking a few questions about what we want the government to do for us, said she was putting together a report for 6PR, so I told her I helped construct the buildings they use now for their broadcasting. Brings back memories, eh Harry?' He turned to Ruth. 'Harry here, you see – Goldilocks, we used to call him – he was the brains of it, really. An engineer. Worked out how to make the whole thing operate.'

Harry shrugged modestly and blew smoke from the corner of his mouth.

'They were good times, eh mate?' Freddie went on. 'We had high hopes then. High hopes.'

Harry remembered well their confidence in a future that would have a fulfilling place for each of them. 'Different story now,' he said sourly, squashing the stub of his cigarette underfoot. 'Relief-gang drudgery for you, empty days at the Canning Bridge camp for me. Quite a comedown.'

They stood there talking for a few minutes. Ruth got Harry to say a little about his training as an engineer, and to reminisce about establishing the wireless station. And how long, she wanted to know, had they been out of work, and how were they trying to make ends meet, and what were conditions like at the Canning Bridge camp, and what did they think about the dole scheme?

'You won't read much about real hardship in the papers,' she said, shaking her head as she jotted down notes. 'I bet they won't give a sympathetic account of today's demonstration, either. But radio can be different. It can bring people's voices directly into other people's homes and let them hear what's actually happening.'

'So you have regular work, paid work, with 6PR?' asked Freddie.

'Oh, no. The station runs on a shoestring. Belongs to Nicholson's, and they don't want to put much money into it in times like these. I've just done a couple of programs, freelance; the payment doesn't amount to much. But I'm getting experience, and with a bit of luck that will land me a job in journalism one day, when the slump is over. Meanwhile I work part-time up at the mental hospital on Point Heathcote, just helping out with the chores. Sad place, but it brings me enough wages to keep body and soul together. I'm lucky to have got a foot in the door at 6PR. My friend Patrick's the technician there and he persuaded the manager to give me a go. Patrick would be really interested in your stories.'

She paused, pondering, and then her eyes widened. 'You know what I'd really like to arrange?' she said. 'I want to get you two in front of a microphone with me, up at the Applecross station. Broadcast an interview where you talk about the old days of building that place, and about the contrast between what you felt then and how things have turned out for you now. About the skills that are going to waste.'

'Nah,' said Freddie. 'Wouldn't feel right to me, somehow, talking to a microphone. Harry's your man for that sort of thing. He's got the poise and the polish.'

'But you'd be talking to us, like the conversation we've just been having. I'd prefer to have both of you there together.'

Freddie pursed his mouth sceptically. She turned to Harry: 'What do you say, Mr Hopewell?'

'Well, you can count me in if Freddie's part of it too.'

Freddie lifted his shoulder in a self-deprecating manner, which Ruth took as consent.

'Monday, then, both of you? Let's say eleven o'clock. The main building on the hill.'

⌒

Back at the Canning Bridge camp, Harry sat out in front of his tent in the late afternoon sunlight, smoking as he read more of the book that he had borrowed from Jim Kirby, *Progress and Poverty*. That land value should be shared as common property: the idea appealed to him, and Henry George's prose had a simple directness. There were several keen readers among the camping families. Misfortune, it seemed to Harry, was making people thoughtful. They wanted to understand what had gone wrong with society, how to cope with its disorder; and they hoped the printed word would tell them – through books, pamphlets, newspaper articles, anything they could lay their hands on. They thirsted not only for political argument and economic analysis but also for the insights that serious novels brought to them: despite being set in unfamiliar places, stories like *Main Street* or *The Good Earth* absorbed their attention because they showed how people could suffer stinging frustration and hardship in ways that made them more resiliently human.

The power of storytelling was something Harry remembered with intense nostalgic pleasure. From the time he was ten or eleven years old, his mother used to read aloud a chapter from a novel after the dishes were cleared from the dinner table. She had a good reading voice and a flair for making words sparkle and shimmer as she lifted them off the page. He and his father used to love the little ritual that drew the three of them together and transported them into an imaginary world. They liked long novels, and Dickens above all. Even when too young to understand some of the language, Harry was entranced by the phantasmagorical parade of characters and events winding through all those mud-strewn alleys and jangling thoroughfares, the houses filled with murk and mould and whispered secrets, the sinuous stretches of mist-shrouded river, and the whole conglomeration of factories, offices, schoolrooms, courtrooms, shops, taverns, banks, workhouses, graveyards, markets, stables, chambers, prisons, that made up the comical but sinister Dickensian circus. As those tales flickered now across the screen of his memory, it seemed to Harry that, more than anything else, what had seized his boyhood imagination was a fearful sense of how family relationships could shift distortedly. In novel after novel, parents acted like children; children acted like parents; siblings turned into strangers; and strangers into siblings.

For the first time in many years he recalled to mind the opening chapters of *Great Expectations*: the piteous spectacle of the orphaned Pip, scanning a list of his grievous losses on the family tombstone, then being grasped by a frightening apparition who turns his filial world upside down, holding him by the ankles, menacing him with dire threats, and releasing him only on terms that require the terrified boy to deceive his surrogate parents. How cruelly misshapen Pip's expectations became, how false was the future he dreamed of with such eagerness, how harmful was the withholding of knowledge about the relationships that formed his sense of who he was!

It was only, Harry thought as he looked back fondly on Collaroy evenings and their simple ceremony of shared storytelling, it was only because his own little family circle was so free of those Dickensian deformities and inversions that he could listen to such tales without being scared witless. Although he'd later come to see that there were things he didn't know about his mother and father, he'd felt sure at the time there were no secrets or clandestine yearnings that might suddenly rear up and come between them. He had grown up with the cloudless confidence that comes from being the eye's apple of parents who seem happily secure in one another's affections.

Eleven

A thick cloud cover made the sky leaden, and beneath it the river had the smooth cold sheen of a slab of galena. Perched on a limestone outcrop high above the strip of beach, he could see near the water's edge little clots of drifting weed and the skeletal shape of a long half-buried boat, which became under his brooding gaze the silt-clogged wreckage of stranded dreams.

With plenty of time on his hands, Harry had left his campsite early, crossed the Canning Bridge and walked along the Swan shoreline past the remains of the Coffee Point slipway. Clambering around the promontory at Point Heathcote, he made his way to its northern side and had paused to rest on this ledge of brittle stone above the wreck that lay there, sunken and sand-chafed. Out to his left was the long grey fringe of the curving bay that stretched past a dilapidated jetty to Point Dundas, where the Majestic Hotel, though past its prime, still dominated the headland.

The Nellie of twenty years ago slid into his reverie again as he sat there above the dead boat's vestigial shell, idly picking stalks of grass and slitting them with a thumbnail. Where was that puckering smile of hers now? If still alive, what might she be doing? What companions would she have? The lilt of an old sentimental melody came to him: if only he could find her, 'Then would all clouds of sorrow depart'. But it was futile, he knew, to slip back recurrently into this spectral nostalgia. He shook his head, stood up, slapped his hat against his thigh, and descended the slope to resume his walk along the riverside. The station was about three miles away. As he approached the eastern part of Point Dundas he turned his back to the water, beginning to wend his way southwest along a bush track towards the wireless mast in the distance. Then came a familiar plaintive call: *kyew kyew kyew*.

He scanned the sky. There it was, superb, moving majestically in a smooth circle: an osprey. It came gliding in his direction, and as it skimmed overhead he could see clearly the white patches under its long arched wings. He whistled to it. The bird tilted its white head and looked straight at him through the dark mask around its eye. Harry remembered an osprey from years ago at Narrabeen Lagoon, how it soared over the still water in search of fish, looked down, and stalled, hovering, hovering, before it swooped steeply, spinning its body to plunge feet first into the water, then climbed the air currents with a wriggly fish grasped in its talons. When he had described this the next day at school his words flapped excitedly around the classroom, and he could see that all the other children were up there too, up with the osprey, feeling the wind whistle past their wings. Their teacher, Mr Prentice, told them that ospreys were not only clever hunters but also strange collectors: they were known, he said, to clutter their nests with all sorts of oddments, a rag doll or a toy sailboat, a blacking brush, an animal bone. 'Like decorating a home,' Harry had called out, and Mr Prentice nodded, smiling. 'Just like that, Harry, yes.'

Crossing Fremantle Road, he paused to look up at the spreading branches of the Moreton Bay Fig, still a small tree when he saw it last; now its thick dark limbs had an almost elephantine appearance. Not far beyond, beside the little road that curved up the hill, was the row of cottages built twenty years ago for the station manager and the telegraphists' families. He wondered whether some of the men he'd known were still there, but he didn't want to see them, didn't want them to see him with his damaged eye and scruffy clothes, didn't want them to know that things had turned out so disappointingly for him. None could have imagined that Goldilocks, the smart young engineer, would be unemployed at the age of forty.

As he made his way up the steep incline to the hilltop station he heard sharp voices calling out.

'Hey! What are you doing up there? Painting the clouds with sunshine?'

'Come back down, mate! That's a bloody dangerous place to be.'

Quickening his pace and approaching the buildings, he saw that several people were peering up at the aerial. There was a stout man away up high, three or four times above roof level, and still climbing the ladder laboriously, ignoring the shouts. As Harry stared up at him, shielding his good eye from the sun, he recognised with a jolt of alarm that the climber was Freddie.

What the hell had got into him? Was this some crazy display of bravado?

'Freddie! It's me, Harry!' he cried out anxiously. 'Don't be a lunatic!' Freddie looked down at him, shook his head, and kept going up. After every few rungs he paused for breath and hitched up his heavy shoulders before pressing on.

Harry started to move towards the foot of the ladder. He would have to go up after the stupid bugger and try to talk him down.

Freddie must have been at least a hundred feet from the ground when he suddenly released his grip, twisted away from the ladder and flung himself outwards into a dive, arms spread wide and hands turned inwards as if embracing nothingness.

The noise as his body hit the earth was thicker than any thud and like nothing Harry had heard before. For a moment no-one moved. Then they all converged, hesitantly, on the corpse. Blood was pooling around the smashed face. One of the onlookers groaned and vomited.

Fists unclenching, Harry wrapped his arms tightly around his ribs as if to protect himself from contagion. He began to shake, and turned away with his head down. This was not a place to linger. As he slowly left the scene, still tremulous, he saw that Ruth stood near the door of the main building, hand over her mouth, sobbing into the shoulder of a young man who had an arm around her. Harry could not bring himself to speak to her or anyone else. He felt ill.

All the way back to the Canning Bridge camp he was in a kind of stupor. That Freddie could have brought his life so abruptly to such a violent end, this man with whom he had worked and laughed and shared drinks and stories, was incomprehensible. What demon had seized Freddie's mind? He'd been down on his luck, of course, and unhappy for a long time – but who'd have guessed he felt so desperately alone that this extreme act of brutal self-extinction seemed the only choice left? Harry shook his head, trying to rid himself of the image and sound of Freddie's body smacking into the ground.

Witnessing the terrible deed was like being struck by a sudden electrical shock. And compounding Harry's anguish were remorseful thoughts about what he might have done to prevent the thing from happening. There must have been some warning sign, he told himself, something he'd failed to notice in Freddie's previous behaviour that carried a faint print of distress, something that Harry should have detected and elicited. He'd been too absorbed in his own shrunken world to notice his friend's state of mind. And if he hadn't been so melancholic that he dawdled on the way to the wireless station, perhaps he could even have arrived in time to avert disaster.

The next day he borrowed a newspaper and searched its pages for information about a funeral. There was a brief item under the heading FATAL FALL AT WIRELESS STATION, but it gave no significant details and made no mention of Freddie's name. The police, said this report, were pursuing enquiries about the background to the man's death.

A couple of days later Harry was sitting outside his tent reading *Progress and Poverty* when a policeman approached.

'Mr Hopewell?'

'That's me.'

'I'm Sergeant Bilson. A lass at the wireless station said I might find you here. I believe you were among the onlookers on Monday when that unfortunate death occurred.'

'I was, yes.'

'And you knew the deceased?'

'I did. Freddie Dingle. Poor sod.'

'What was your own personal connection with him, Mr Hopewell?'

'We were pretty close at times. Got on well. He was one of the men who built the station twenty years ago,' Harry explained, 'and I worked there too in those days. We lost touch for years but I caught up with him again just recently and we talked a bit.'

'Any idea why he killed himself?'

'Can't quite understand it, really. I didn't ever take his jokey manner at face value – there was something a bit deeper – but I hadn't seen this coming. Being unemployed for so long must have hit him harder than I'd have thought. And I suppose being abandoned, that's how he saw it, by his wife.'

'Know where we can contact her, or any of his family members?'

'Can't help with that, no. He and his wife were living apart, but I don't know where she is now. I think perhaps she may have had relatives up Guildford way, if I remember rightly.'

'You don't know anything about his involvement in anyone else's death?'

Harry looked at him with wordless astonishment – and then with consternation, as a dreadful thought gripped him.

The sergeant handed him an envelope with 'Harry Hopewell' written on it.

'We found this in Mr Dingle's pocket.'

Harry grabbed the envelope, noticing that the flap had already been opened, and pulled out a sheet of paper that was closely written on both sides.

Harry, there's something I've been badly needing to get off my chest and in the last few days I've come to decide you're the only person I can tell.

A long time ago I did a terrible thing that I just can't keep buried any longer. It's been tormenting me more and more, so this is the only way of stopping the thoughts. I took someone's life once, and I've been too cowardly to own up. Then because I kept silent, a second person died, too. So now I want to be my own executioner.

It was me that killed Doris Biddle, the poor wretch. I wish to God I'd never laid eyes or hands on her, it just happened, I didn't plan it. I hadn't touched any woman's flesh for a year or more, my wife wouldn't let me near her, and I was full of frustration, and bitterness too, and rage and lust. That particular evening after another row at home I went for a walk, moody as hell, and there was young Doris out by herself in the twilight, and we struck up conversation. I persuaded her to stroll with me down Como way, to have a look at the yachts moored near the jetty. In the darkness one thing led to another. I got all fired up but she resisted and I had to stop her yelling out, and in the struggle I wrapped her belt around her neck and she suffocated. That put me in a real panic, so I dragged her along the jetty and shoved her off the side of it and then hurried back home, scared we might have been seen together, but apparently not. Then, after her body was found, people needed a culprit and suspicion fell on that sad old bugger Fritz, conveniently for me, so I kept quiet. What they did to him, though – I never imagined anyone would do something like that. No idea who bashed him, but I've got his blood on my hands as much as Doris's blood. All these years their voices have been accusing me in my head. I didn't set out to hurt either of them. And then there was the way it affected her parents, too. I don't deserve to be alive.

P.S. I had nothing to do with your Nellie's disappearance, believe me.

'Nothing further you can tell us about this matter?' the policeman asked, holding out his hand for the piece of paper.

Shaking his head, Harry put the note back in the envelope and gave it to him without a word. There was a roiling sensation in his gut, as if water from around the Como jetty had begun to slosh inside him. He tried to steady his breathing as the sergeant left. His feelings were raw, diffuse, shapeless.

At the twilight end of a quiet afternoon a few weeks later, he was fishing from the side of Canning Bridge when a strolling couple stopped beside him. He turned to see that it was Ruth Grace and the young man who had comforted her at the scene of Freddie's suicide.

'This is my friend, Patrick,' she told him.

'I remember you, Mr Hopewell,' said Patrick as they shook hands. 'Not very well, I admit. We used to live under the same roof for a while.'

'Really? When was that?' asked Harry, taken aback.

'Oh, before the war. About twenty years ago, must have been; I was just a nipper, not more than five or six years old, but I remember the names of our boarders. I'm Patrick Riven, you see. My parents ran the boarding house where you stayed.'

'Astonishing! It seems so long ago. How are your parents?'

'Passed away within a few months of each other a couple of years back.'

Harry murmured some sympathetic words.

'I'm glad we've run into you, Mr Hopewell,' said Ruth. 'About that interview we were going to do: despite the...the horrible incident that day – and I'm so sorry: losing your friend in such a shocking way must have been...I don't know what to say – but I still want to go ahead, if you're willing, and talk with you on air about the early days of wireless. The two of us. Next Monday, perhaps? Could you meet me at the station up there a bit before eleven? Yes?'

He nodded wryly. 'Nothing much else in my social diary.'

Monday morning came and he walked to the station in a sombre mood. But Ruth's questions soon made reminiscence easy and the microphone drew words from him readily, restoring some of the pleasure that conversation used to give him in his youth. Being on air and recalling what had been done here in earlier days: there was satisfaction in that. The world of wireless had turned out to be even more expansive than he could have imagined when he first set foot on the hill.

Months passed after that broadcast, and he gave no further thought to 6PR or Ruth until, as he walked aimlessly one sun-scorched January afternoon through the dusty streets of Como, he saw her coming towards him with Patrick Riven beside her again.

Hand in hand, they greeted him warmly.

'Small world!' she said, and added as if unaware of his threadbare jacket and scruffy old shirt, 'How are you getting on?'

Harry shrugged and managed a crooked smile.

Then Patrick blurted, 'We've got some news, Mr Hopewell.' Harry looked from one to another. 'We're engaged to be married,' Ruth told him.

He shook their hands vigorously and said the expected cheerful things, and in truth the shimmer of their happiness made him, for the moment, almost happy too. There they were, all grins, sharing the prospect of a companionable future: he could hardly begrudge them that good fortune, and he pushed away the flickering ghost of self-pity.

They chatted for a few minutes about this and that, hands shielding their faces from the sun. The whine of a small biplane in the northern sky caught their attention.

'That's the future!' Harry exclaimed, peering and pointing. 'Down here it's all struggle, but up there a few ingenious spirits are looking further than our horizon. Hope on the wing, eh! You heard about Smithy and his crew last week? Crossed the Tasman for the second time! Amazing achievement.'

Ruth shook her head. 'Why do they take such risks? Even the cleverest aviators seem to be dicing with death. There was that sad news just the other day about Hinkler's disappearance on his latest solo flight from England. Still no sign of him, so he must have crashed.'

In a sidelong flutter of memory, Harry could hear Nellie voicing much the same sentiment in much the same tone when they were walking together near this spot so long ago. And he began to echo things he had said to Nellie on that occasion, expressing now to Ruth and Patrick, more and more volubly as the old fervour surged again, something of the wondrous appeal that aviation still had for those who once witnessed its earliest endeavours.

'Bert Hinkler's exactly my age, you see,' he told her. 'He's done the things I always wanted to do. Same as mine, his love of flying started when he was just a boy, watching a glider skimming over a beach.' And he told them about that happy day at Narrabeen Heads when he saw the Taylors make their historic series of flights.

'But flying has changed so much!' he went on, gesticulating. 'Tremendous advances since those days. Engines – the power of them now!'

His eye glistened with renewed enchantment. Browning's words, long dormant, stirred in his mind: 'successive zones of several wonder'. And there was another phrase he couldn't quite recall: something about a flying spirit.

Ruth smiled in a way that made him feel they had known one another for a long time. 'We'll have to arrange another radio interview with you,' she said. 'No, I mean it, seriously. I'd love to get you talking about travelling through the air. By air, whatever the right expression is. Listeners would find it fascinating, I'm sure they would, to hear about that experience you had as a boy, watching the glider lift up over the beach.'

'Perhaps,' said Harry, pretending nonchalance. When she pressed him he agreed to go again to the hilltop studio, and they arranged a time.

But his mood began to sag as he walked back towards the Canning Bridge camp. What he had been saying so effusively to Ruth and Patrick about wireless and aviation and an adventurous horizon – it was all true, he did believe that; but as far as he could see, such a bright prospect held no place for him. His life had stalled.

It was a summer that seemed to stretch endlessly, with unremitting heat day after day. In the long evenings down near the river, men sat listlessly in singlets outside their tents and humpies, cursing and swatting at the mosquitoes that cigarette or pipe smoke could not deter. Not many yards away the Canning moved silently towards its convergence with the Swan. Even this far up from the sea there was a faint tidal flux, and though unseen in the twilight it seemed almost as perceptible to Harry as the tugging of his own heart's current.

He listened quietly to the chatter.

'Certain to be a change of government here. No doubt of that,' Jim Kirby reckoned.

'But it wouldn't bring much improvement anyway,' said Bill Sewell. 'Look at what happened with the Federal Labor government. Hopeless.'

'Well, Labor under Collier will soon get things moving again in this state,' Jim retorted.

'You make Collier sound like a dose of Senna tea.'

'Very funny, Bill, but look here: you ought to wake your ideas up by reading some of the articles in the *Westralian Worker*. Or listening to some of the political speeches they're broadcasting on 6PR. I've got a friend in Como with a crystal set; how about we drop in on him one of these evenings to hear what reformers like John Curtin are saying on the air waves?'

'Perhaps,' said Bill, 'but I'll have to ask one of my secretaries to check on whether I've got any time to spare. And anyway,' he added, 'tuning a crystal set to receive a politician's words is using a cat's whisker to subject yourself to a windbag who thinks he's a full kit of cat's whiskers.'

And so the chiacking went on around him while Harry kept his thoughts to himself, watched the fading of the light, and felt his future slowly ebb away.

Part 3

1938 – 1939

Twelve

As they continued to lose altitude, the engine's groan became alarmingly plangent. Even before one of the propellers began to lose power, there seemed little chance of keeping above the snowy ridges. The mountainside came rushing towards them and a violent impact flung them from their seats. In the sudden silence that followed, Conway picked himself up and looked around the cabin. It was miraculously intact. The other passengers stirred, moving their limbs charily, and to their amazement none of them seemed to be hurt.

Watching it all happen on the distant screen below as he peered through the small window up in the hot projection box, Harry had involuntarily clenched his sweaty hands at the moment of the crash, though he knew, having sat through this first part of the movie twice before, that they would come to no harm. The survivors would be led through ice and snow to the hidden Tibetan utopia, Shangri-la, whose wonders would gradually be disclosed to them. But each time, Harry's trance was broken before the action unfolded further:

the first reel would finish, and it was his job to take it speedily from one picture theatre to the other in a basket fixed to the handlebars of his bike. Canny Jim Stiles, owner of both the Gaiety and the Hurlingham, always timed the sessions so that a single print would suffice for the pair of screenings. Harry was glad of his fetch-and-carry role. It brought in a few shillings a week, and allowed him to see portions of each film free of charge. He owed the arrangement to young Patrick Riven, who had left 6PR about a year ago to become projectionist at the Gaiety. Harry's work as Patrick's helper was menial, yes, but after so long without any steady employment he was grateful for it.

To Harry, it seemed less important to know every component of the plot than just to let images, phrases, personages and associations drift slowly across his mind. *Lost Horizon*: this film's wistful title was streaked with hope and melancholy together, and its main character combined different selves, the pragmatic man of action and the romantic dreamer. In Robert Conway, Harry recognised something of the person he once thought he himself would become – inventive, accomplished, decisive – mingled with the lesser person he now felt himself to be, epitomising disappointment. And as he pedalled along Suburban Road with the reel tin rattling in the basket and scenes from the film replaying in his head, two little details about the story troubled him. One was that, although Conway and his companions had travelled by air into the Himalayas, they could only be led to Shangri-la itself when the plane failed them and they left its wreckage behind. The other was that this imagined paradise lay beyond the reach of wireless, and had no use for it. So the pair of inventions that had inspired

Harry since his youthful days, lighting up a new vista of human progress, simply didn't belong in the utopian world of Shangri-la. It was a disconcerting irony that a vision of such ultimate contentment had left both air travel and radio communication far behind, discarded, lost back there over some forlorn horizon.

~

Warmed by steaming stew and a glowing fireplace, they forgot about the racket of rain on the iron roof and began to talk about all the changes happening around the district over the last few years.

'Walking in South Perth these days, you'd hardly know there'd been a Depression,' said Patrick. 'New cinemas, churches, schools, a fire station, and the population just keeps growing. All that reclamation work going on along the foreshore, too – you should go down there, Harry, to have a look. They've nearly finished filling in the market garden area beyond the jetty, and even Miller's Pool now.'

Harry nodded. He didn't hear much any more about job losses, hardship, a stagnant economy. For most of the people he knew, the tide had turned; that was a fact. But his own fortunes remained at low ebb, and he couldn't stop himself from saying so.

'I suppose it's a kind of progress. Makes things a bit tougher, though, for those of us who've been left behind by it all and can't catch up.' He heard the tinge of bitterness in his tone. 'Don't get me wrong,' he added as Ruth began to clear away the plates. 'I'm grateful for the work you've found for me, Patrick, you know that. Really grateful. And to be boarding here with you – well, you've made me feel so welcome it's almost like being an adopted family member. Very kind. But I just can't get used to…to the fact that nothing has worked out for me the way I thought it would when I was your age.' He paused, shook his head as if trying to rid himself of a tenacious little midge of misery. 'Embarrassing when a bloke starts to feel sorry for himself, eh?'

He ran his fingers through his hair and rubbed his chin. The others looked away and said nothing. Wiping her hands on her apron, Ruth got up to pour cups of tea while Patrick stirred sparks from the fire with a poker and tipped some more lumps from the coal bucket. Harry's maudlin words were making them uncomfortable, that was obvious; but he persisted.

'You never think, when you're young, that accidental things can shape so much of your life.'

Yet mischance, he knew, was only part of the story. He smacked his palm against this thigh, annoyed with himself. It was too easy to see yourself as fate's hapless victim, much harder to acknowledge the possibility of a fault in your own character that let you succumb to circumstance. Something close to shame twisted in his gut.

'Two of sugar, isn't it?'

'Thanks.' He took the cup that Ruth handed to him and blew on the tea to cool it.

'It seemed to be a luckless time for a lot of other people, too,' he went on. 'Luckless and listless, what with the war and then the period after that, when so many were still in a state of shock. Men coming back home from the trenches with terrible injuries, and not just to their bodies. Dispirited men, bewildered, their heads and hearts full of things they couldn't forget but couldn't talk about to their womenfolk. Crippled families. I saw too much of that.'

There was a fretful mewling noise from the other room. Ruth went off to check on the baby and brought her back swaddled in a crocheted shawl. With her free hand, Ruth held up the golliwog cloth doll – Harry's gift – and waggled it across her daughter's line of sight. Grizzles turned to gurgles.

'How about that? Instant soothing!' laughed Ruth. 'Good choice of present, Harry.' The way her mouth creased merrily at its corners brought a smile to his own lips.

'If it works that well I'd better get one for myself!' said Harry, making an effort to discard his melancholy shadow.

'Want to give Rachel a cuddle?' Ruth took the infant over to him. Harry put down his teacup, made a cradle of his arms and held the bundle gingerly against his chest.

'First time in my life I've been this close to a baby,' he said. 'Forty-five years old, and I've never had one in my arms before now.' Tender regret rippled through him. 'Seeing young parents with their newborn – it's a bit of a novelty for me. Come to think of it, this is the only family home I've been invited into for a long while now.'

And in truth he found it touching, their warmth towards him. After the radio interview with Ruth more than five years back, he had encountered them from time to time and they always seemed glad to talk. He wondered at first whether they just felt sorry for him, but the friendly attitude seemed genuine. Then they had invited him to their wedding: a small occasion, because there were no siblings or living parents on either side, just a few friends. Since that simple ceremony he had become at their insistence a frequent visitor to the snug little place they were renting, three-and-a-half back rooms divided off from the rest of someone's shabby weatherboard cottage down near the mill. And now he was living here. For just a couple of quid a week, too.

'We're glad of your company, Harry. Now that the baby keeps me home so much of the time,' she added, 'I miss being out and about, mixing with people. It wasn't easy, you know, to give up my sessions at 6PR and the Heathcote work. I'd love to get back to freelance reporting when Rachel reaches school age. But it's still a man's world, journalism, except for the gossipy Ladies' Page. Plenty of women's voices on radio now, but a lot of the programs are hardly more than idle chatter. As for magazines, well I suppose the *Women's Weekly* shouldn't be sneezed at: it does employ some female journalists, and yes, they do occasionally produce good topical articles, but still there's not much there that interests me. You know what I really admire? It's the kind of commitment to serious writing that you see in a person like Katharine Prichard. She's uncompromising! Not just fearless political reportage, but social realist novels too. You're looking blank, Harry. Haven't read any of her books?'

'Prichard?' Harry shook his head. 'Never heard of her, I confess.'

'Quite famous. Lives up in the hills at Greenmount. She's controversial, forthright, left-wing – communist, in fact. We've got a copy of her latest novel. Like to borrow it?'

She went to a corner of the room where a row of books sat on a low brick-and-plank shelf, and handed one of them to Harry. 'Here – *Intimate Strangers*, it's called. It's about an Australian middle-class couple and how the Depression overturns their comfortably shallow life.'

'So it's not just a book for female readers?'

'Not at all. It held Patrick's attention, didn't it dear?'

'Yes, it's certainly well written. I'll be interested to know what you think of the political side of the story, Harry. I'm less enthusiastic than Ruth about the author, though. As a person, I mean.'

'Why's that?' Harry asked.

'Well, about five or six years ago, when the Depression was at its worst, she went on some bolshie writers' jaunt to Russia: left her husband behind on the farm at Greenmount to cope with their debts and worries, and the poor lonely bugger got into a state of despair and killed himself. There was plenty of talk about it at the time. He was a war hero, you see – won the VC at Gallipoli. Jim Throssell, a local man, good bloke. It was selfish of her to put her own interests ahead of her family.'

'That's unfair, Patrick,' remonstrated Ruth. 'We can't know the whole story. You're just repeating pub tattle. Why lay the blame on her? If you're going to call her selfish, what's your verdict on him? A lot of people would say suicide is a coward's way out, especially when it means leaving a wife to solve your financial problems and bring up your child on her own. But I say cast no stones. No-one outside a family has any right to pass judgement on what goes on within it.'

'OK, Ruth. All the same, you can't put those things completely out of your mind when you're reading her novel. I won't spoil it for you, Harry, but you'll find the plot has some similarities with the Throssell story, and I reckon that raises a few troubling questions.'

They left the matter there, and over a steamed suet pudding their conversation turned to the reporting of international events. The rank cruelty in Nanking and the news of Japanese soldiers rampaging through China – 'like ferocious animals', according to the local paper – was making Australians anxious.

'It's a worry, all right,' said Harry. 'The ring of coastal radio stations we set up years ago could still help to monitor ship movements, but it'd be next to useless now that aircraft travel so far and so fast. Look at the devastation the Jap bomber planes have brought to Chinese cities. Think what they could do to Perth if they came this far.'

Patrick frowned. 'Why would they want to bother with Australia?'

'Simple. We've got big iron ore deposits, but our government doesn't seem able to make up its mind about whether to sell the stuff to the Japs or not. It's not long since Joe Lyons banned iron exports from Australia, and yet now Menzies has tried to bring in strikebreakers because the wharfies refuse to load pig iron being sold to Japan. Their steel mills need to be fed – for manufacturing munitions, among other things. If we don't trade with the Japs they'll come and take what they want.'

Dishes washed and wiped, they talked on until the glow from the fireplace faded. After turning in, Harry found it hard to sleep. He lay on his back and stared into the darkness. The tide of events swirling through Europe and Asia was making him deeply uneasy. People said there would be another world war before long. Had there been anything like this sense of doom in the years before the Great War, when he first came to Perth? This irresistible undertow, this terrible suction? If so, he had been oblivious to it; in those days he was aware only of a cheerful idealism about mankind's future, buoyed by wonderful technical advances.

The 1930s had brought a different world into being, a darker and meaner world. Over a year ago, when the news of Marconi's death came through, it was as if the spirit of an earlier period had died with him. Radio operators all over the globe had shut down their transmitters for two minutes of silence. Was this simply out of respect for the man, or was it also that they mourned the passing of his era's hopefulness? During the thirty years since Marconi began to imagine what wireless could do, it had changed many things; but not all for the better. It could serve the purposes of war as readily as those of peace.

Lying awake, Harry thought of other deaths and of what had passed away with them. His parents, the small local world they knew, their simple pride in him, the affectionate home where he had grown up. And then several people, now gone, who had been part of the community around him in South Perth before the war: Doris Biddle and her parents, old Fritz, Freddie Dingle. Nellie too: though perhaps still alive somewhere, she was no longer alive to him. And old Le Souef had died a few months back, having retired as director of the zoo when the Depression struck. Harry remembered clearly, as if it were in a family portrait, Le Souef and the orangutan with their arms around each other's shoulders and their heads inclining together.

Thirteen

Whistling and snuffling, the steam locomotive chugged its asthmatic way underneath the new road bridge at Clackline. In Harry's carriage there were only half a dozen passengers, but pungent tobacco smoke, blending with whiffs of sooty engine exhaust, had filled it even before the train began its slow climb up into the Darling escarpment. A pale youth across the aisle, frowning with concentration, would carefully roll himself another cylinder while the one that hung precariously from his lip became shorter, and light it with the stub's last glow, repeating the sequence each time as if arranging a continuous relay of little torches.

Harry had kept a pipe in his mouth throughout the journey, but left it unlit. Having something to clamp his teeth on was making it easier for him to cut back on smoking. The habit was getting too expensive. Today he intended to keep right off cigarettes. He'd smoke just a couple tomorrow, rolling his own with the coarse-cut pipe tobacco that gave his lungs a good kick. Small embers had left scorch holes down the front of his shirt.

Facing Harry in the seat opposite, a swarthy bearded man with a face like dry cracked leather and a strange little hat perched on his head had pulled a mouth organ from his jacket at the previous water stop. Hands cupped protectively around his noisy sucking and puffing, he produced a warbled approximation of 'You are My Sunshine' and then 'Smoke Gets in Your Eyes'.

'You like?' he asked with a gap-toothed grin as he put the instrument back in his pocket. Harry nodded. 'More later,' the man promised, or threatened. 'What you do?' he wanted to know. Harry put on a vaguely uncomprehending look. So the man – Italian, could he be, or Yugoslav perhaps? – pursued his inquisition: 'Your home, it's not up around here somewhere, eh? Then where you going what for?'

Harry took the pipe from his mouth. 'Oh, I see what you mean. Well, I'm really just looking for a decent job around Northam, maybe, or further afield. Been living in the city, y'see, but nothing much suits me down there. If I find something in these parts that pays OK, I'll probably settle down for a while.'

'What you like?'

'Oh, can't be too choosy. If it gives me a good wage I'll take it, within reason. Not much chance of getting to do the things I'd really like to do.'

The swarthy fellow raised his eyebrows histrionically and opened his hands, miming an invitation to tell him more.

'What kind of work would I most like to get?' Harry turned his head away for a moment and looked out through the carriage window at the sandy paddocks and tattered trees.

'Not sure any more, to be honest, but I'll tell you what first got me interested in the idea of coming up this way, though I know there's no work attached to it now. Have you heard about Selby Ford and his homemade aeroplane? The Silver Centenary, he called it. Doesn't ring a bell? Well, I read about it a long while back, and it's an amazing bloody contraption. They've had it in mothballs for years, but I'd love to clap eyes on it. Ford was a brilliant amateur, you see. Knew nothing about aerodynamics but he'd been up in a joy flight a few years earlier and he became fascinated with the idea of flying. Lived not far from here – still does, I think – in Beverley, where he owned the town's powerhouse. So when he got the idea of building a biplane for the state's centenary celebrations, he just sketched his plans for it in chalk on the floor of the powerhouse! Then he made templates from the plans, and got the local butcher to help him build the timber frame. And the butcher's sister, I think it was, sewed all the fabric for covering it.'

The foreign bloke interrupted. 'All true, this story?'

'All true, mate. Well, it had got to 1929 by this time, and luck brought them the vital component when a plane in a Centenary Air Race crashed nearby. Ford managed to buy the undamaged engine. By the middle of the next year everything was ready, so they arranged for an experienced pilot to give it a burl. They reckon most of the town turned out to watch the plane being towed from the powerhouse along the main street of Beverley to a local paddock, and it not only flew successfully but went up several more times before the day was over, with passengers. Caused a stir, all right. They had more flights for the next few months but then Selby found out that the plane was only licensed for restricted experimental flying. He tried to get a full licence but he didn't have proper blueprints and stress charts and whatnot. And he couldn't give them the chalk marks on the powerhouse floor! Well, the authorities wouldn't give him the certificate, so he strung the plane up from the ceiling of his powerhouse and I heard it's been there ever since. I'd love to see it, I really would. A little monument to ingenuity, eh!'

As Harry paused, the pallid young man across the aisle said quietly from one side of his mouth, without taking the cigarette from the other side, 'I was there when it went up.'

Harry turned towards him. 'What – you mean you saw the Silver Centenary in flight?'

'Yep. I grew up in Beverley,' the smoker said, stub jiggling precariously now on his nether lip as he spoke. 'The word had got around, see, that Mr Ford was building this machine, and then the big day arrived for trying it out. Everyone knew. I was still at school but our teacher let us out so we could watch. We all cheered when they wheeled her out of the powerhouse into the street, and we followed along to Benson's paddock, and a pilot bloke, Captain somebody, he got in and started her up and away she went, circled around overhead for the best part of half an hour. Most exciting thing I've ever seen.' The memory of such gleefulness seemed to make him shy and he retreated behind a cloud of smoke.

Harry broke the silence. 'What a shame, though,' he said, 'not to be able to get it licensed. Imagine if any of the earliest aviators, the pioneers, had needed an airworthy certificate for their planes before they could fly.' Or, he thought, if I'd had to get official permission to improvise the receiver equipment for the wireless station at Applecross.

He turned to the swarthy bloke. 'You live up this way somewhere yourself?' The Italian man nodded, or Yugoslav, or whatever he was. From Albania, perhaps.

'Near Northam. Working for a farmer, Mr Lawrence. Rouseabout. I help with everything. He gives me meals and I sleep in the shed. Is all right. Is good life. Peace and quiet, peace and quiet. Not like Boulder.'

'Boulder?'

'The riots. I was there, 1934. The big fighting that happened, you know? Britisher miners, they attacked us in Kalgoorlie, then in Boulder. They throw bombs and smash up our houses and shops. For nothing. Shoot to death my friend Jo Katich, good man, hard worker, never doing wrong things. They said we pay bribes to the shift bosses to get best work. But never we did, never.'

He paused and shook his head.

'I heard a bit about the rioting,' said Harry. 'In Perth a lot of unemployed men were made special constables and sent by train to Kalgoorlie to calm things down, I remember that. But I didn't know what really happened out there.'

'It started up for nothing, no reason, the fighting. Before was friendly, we played in same football teams, went to same churches. But after the riots, no. Turn on us suddenly like wild animals. So I left Boulder.'

As he had done now each evening for the last month, Harry stood in the shed doorway smoking, peering out into the dusk. He allowed himself one cigarette after tea; there was comfort and calmness in this simplest of rituals performed while he listened to the sounds drifting from paddocks and the distant road. Sporadic lowing and bleating. The fading sputter of some engine. The verdict of a sullen crow: *Dark, dark, nark.*

Crushing the stub underfoot, he went over to his bunk and stretched out on the lumpy kapok mattress. The only noise inside the shed was the occasional slap of playing cards on the little pine butter-box that Goran used as a table for his games of patience. Harry knew without looking that, in the candlelight, Goran would be a portrait of concentration, leaning forward intently and setting the cards down with a fixed frown as if his fortune depended on the outcome.

It was thanks to Goran that Harry had found work.

'You come along with me,' he'd said. 'Many things for doing around the farm already now, and soon it will be November harvest. Mr Lawrence, he is looking for good workers. Very fair boss. He keeps my job while I see my sick brother in Perth.'

By the time their train reached Northam, they had arranged to hitch a ride together from the rail station. A local truck driver took them as far as the Grass Valley hotel and then they walked south. With the late afternoon sun at his right shoulder and swinging an old suitcase, Harry felt a current of something close to cheerfulness, and began to whistle 'Camptown Races'. He hoped Goran was right, and that the farmer wouldn't turn him away. He wasn't worried, though. Even if there was no work going, surely he'd be allowed to doss down in the shed overnight, and then he could make his way back to Northam and try his luck in the town. But Mr Lawrence didn't hesitate to offer him a job – 'for two or three months, at least.' So here he was now, liking the work outdoors, looking forward to the harvesting, sleeping well at nights.

Letting his thoughts flow randomly through the quietness, he pictured Selby Ford's plane, hoisted to the rafters of the

Beverley powerhouse and gathering dust. A sorry outcome, yet the man's feat of inventiveness was undiminished. What a thrill he must have felt as the thing he'd imagined and built began to lift high into the air.

Few things matched the satisfaction of devising a clever homemade solution to a big problem. Harry remembered passages in *The Home of the Blizzard* that showed how resourceful Mawson and his mates were in putting together all sorts of makeshift arrangements with limited materials. Their ingenuity was admirable. When the wireless mast broke and the wind was too fierce for repairs to be done immediately, they constructed a box-kite to serve as a temporary aerial. When they decided to measure the velocity of heavy gusts, they came up with their own 'puffometer', a contrivance that used a light cord to attach a small aluminium sphere to a recording instrument so that when the winds caught the sphere it exerted tension on a calibrated spring and transferred it to a lever carrying a pencil across a slowly revolving disk of carbonised paper. Bloody remarkable.

Those were feats of practical intelligence in extreme conditions. But ordinary people could sometimes come up with impressive little engineering solutions too. He remembered his own proud moment a quarter of a century ago at the Applecross wireless station, when he managed to fix the malfunctioning reception equipment. He'd experienced nothing so satisfying since then.

As he lay on his bunk, his thoughts drifted to the young friends he'd regretfully parted from in Perth, Patrick and Ruth. In the months spent boarding with them he'd got to know them both well, and in the evenings they'd spoken freely about many things. Fresh in his mind now was a particular conversation not long before he left to look for work in the Wheatbelt. Somehow Ruth had got him talking about his early years in Collaroy, and about his parents. So then he'd asked what happened to her family.

'I never knew them. My mother must have died in childbirth, and someone said they thought my father was a fallen soldier. Nuns in Bunbury brought me up from infancy and they gave me the name Ruth. They said they had no information for me about my parents. That's what they told me, anyway. For the first few years I was looked after at the convent – Sisters of Mercy. And then I was sent to the little Catholic school at Greenbushes, out Bridgetown way, and later on to St Joseph's Orphanage up in Subiaco. Nearest I got to being part of a family.'

Ruth had spoken calmly but Harry felt at the time, and felt again now as he remembered what she had said, the pang of that deep absence in her life. Not to know one's parents – not to know what they looked like, how they sounded; not to be able to remember any particular thing that one's mother or father had done – it must produce a sense of deprivation. No echoes of songs sung in the home, not even fragments of family stories.

Goran was still engrossed in his solitary card game. Harry lit another candle and pulled out from his wallet an old cherished letter, the last one received from his mother. The date was almost exactly twelve years ago. She had written to say she was dying. He held her words close to the candlelight.

'It's not so much the dying, Harry. I don't feel an old woman yet, and would dearly like to last longer, but I had thirty good years with Jim, and I'm proud to have you as our son. As I write these words now, I'm looking at two photographs of you near the beginning of your life. In one of them you're just a newborn babe: your dad is holding you carefully, looking anxious, as if you had the frailty of a butterfly, though in fact you were a sturdy little thing from the start, nearly ten pounds birth-weight! The second picture's dated on the back, so I know it shows you at exactly two and a half, with those curls framing your face like a frilly wimple, and you're clutching my skirt with one hand while in the other hand there's a scrap of paper – call me fanciful but it almost seems like a little text you've written for yourself, a secret script with directions for the road ahead!

'Well, you've travelled a long way since then, son, and achieved a lot. It upsets me that I'll never find out what will happen to you. Or to your Aunt Muriel, and our friends, everyone. I just wish I could know how all the stories will end. What you're going to do next, Harry, with those talents of yours. What kind of girl you'll choose to marry. (Don't leave it too much longer!) What your children will be like. Where your family eventually settles down, and how it all turns out.

'Facing death must be quite different, I suppose, for people like the Moncriefs next door, with their religious faith. As you know, your dad and I have always rejected that kind of consolation. Perhaps there may be some kind of afterlife, but I just can't believe it would allow me to watch what happens to you – follow the story of your life. So I'll never know. Sad to say.'

Folding the creased and faded letter, he wasn't sorry that she didn't know. It would have distressed her to find out how his life had dwindled into an anti-climax.

And besides, while his mother didn't know how things had turned out for him, there were also gaps in his own knowledge of her life story. He'd heard a few tales from her childhood and growing up, but she had never told him much about the years between leaving school and meeting his father. He knew that she was in her mid-twenties when they married, but couldn't remember any mention of what she had been doing before that.

Fourteen

'Sorry,' he said. 'Can't help it.'

'It doesn't matter,' she said. 'It's all right. But just don't talk about it. I need to turn you over now.'

He wanted to tell her: If a young woman pulls down a bloke's pyjama pants, even in the line of duty, she can hardly expect his flesh to stay inert.

Anyway, the awkwardness of this bed-wash routine, mixed with the stirrings of concupiscence, did at least stop him from being wholly preoccupied with his injuries. He felt grateful for any physical sensation that could distract him even for a few minutes. With both arms and one leg in splints, and a big bandage around his head, he didn't need to be told that he was going to be helplessly confined to this bed for a long while. One arm lay across his chest, strapped down to immobilise shoulder and collarbone; the other was stretched out rigidly, the splint extending to his fingertips. He couldn't do a thing for himself, even scratch his nose, adjust his position, drink a glass of water.

Sidelong, he glanced at her. There seemed to be a slight blush at her neckline. She wasn't what you could call beautiful, not by any means, but she looked very agreeable, this young nurse. He liked her voice, too, and her quiet, gentle manner of attending to all the patients.

'Your badge just says Nurse Watkins,' he said. 'It doesn't tell me your first name.'

'Elva,' she told him shyly. He liked the sound of it. 'But you should call me Nurse,' she added with a belated nod towards professional propriety.

During the slow daily ritual through which he was undressed, turned, sponged, rinsed, patted dry and powdered, they gradually exchanged pieces of their stories. These little narrative transactions made him feel less passive, and he supposed she was glad to have something to take her mind off the tedium of conducting his protracted ablutions. With curtains drawn around his bed and no-one nearby in the half-empty ward, they could talk quietly without disturbing others. The process began with his casual questions about how and why she became a nurse. Her motivation was simple, Elva said: as the eldest of five children, with a chronically ill mother, she had grown up taking care of her siblings through their various bouts of sickness, doing most of the housework, and tending their mother in the final stages of a piteous struggle against the throat cancer that carried her off; and so, after all that, the choice of nursing seemed just a way of extending formally what had already turned out to be her natural vocation. As for the subsequent training in Perth, she had enjoyed nearly every minute of it. 'Especially,' she added, and her giggle hinted at mischief, 'playing with the anatomical dummy.'

'Tell me more, Elva.' He declined to call her Nurse. Her name felt pleasant on his tongue.

'Ah well, as probationers, you see, before we were allowed to do anything in the wards, we had to spend a month receiving what they called preliminary instruction. We learnt how to make poultices, apply dressings, practise bandaging, that type of thing. They couldn't let us loose on real patients, so we had a pair of life-size dummies to show the body's internal workings. One male, one female. Quite realistic actually. You'd lift off the outer parts to reveal the vital organs. Each bit had a number linked to names on a printed list. So there they were, jointed right down to the fingertips, a couple of big bed-ridden dolls, with rubber tubes inside leading from their orifices to waterproof bags, which you could withdraw through a little door in the back of the figure.'

She reached for a couple of small towels. 'Lift your head, can you, just for a moment?' Easing one of the towels under Harry's head, she sluiced some water through his hair, and rubbed off some of the moisture with the other towel.

'Anyway, one of the trainee nurses, this was my friend June, took a special interest in a certain part of the male doll's anatomy because she'd never seen a naked man. Had no brothers. She was quite frank: she simply wanted to know how much a droopy little thing like that would change, so to speak – you know, what it would grow into – to be able to do its duty in…let's say in an amorous situation. Well, that evening I had a bit of time to myself, so I covered a very big long balloon with papier-mâché and painted it a sort of puce colour, and then next morning before the other girls arrived for the day's classes I attached this whopping rigid thing to the dummy and tied a white ribbon bow around it. You can imagine the reaction. But what I didn't expect is that in the midst of all the shrieks of laughter the matron would arrive, and she nearly had an apoplexy. Luckily for me, she stormed out of the room immediately – I think she was too shocked to know what to say; and by the time she gathered her thoughts and returned, we'd all vowed to stick to the line that we had no idea who'd done this. Saved my bacon! I'm sure I'd have been expelled from nursing if she found out I was the culprit.'

She pulled up his pyjama pants and buttoned the jacket. 'There you are. Fresh as a daisy.'

'Not as fresh as I'd like to get after hearing that story,' he said, 'if I wasn't a prisoner in my bed.'

'Now you behave yourself, Mr Hopewell,' she said. 'No flirting.' But he saw her smile as she turned her head away.

Bit by bit, as the days and nights passed, he related the recent phases of his own story. How he'd found it hard to get a decent job in the city. How he'd heard you could get good seasonal employment on Wheatbelt farms, now that machines were displacing regular all-year-round farm workers but still needed men to operate them when the crops ripened. How he'd met up with Goran on the train and then been hired by Mr Lawrence for a three-month period, not only to help with some late harvesting but also to take on miscellaneous tasks around the place – look after the horses, trap rabbits, fix a problem with the tractor, rake the dung from the stables, thatch a new machinery shed, stack the superphosphate bags ready for later use, and put up new fencing on the small neighbouring property that Lawrence had bought for converting to crops when the butter factory closure made dairying unprofitable.

With an engineer's enthusiasm for mechanical details, Harry described to Elva the pair of tractors used on Lawrence's farm. The old Emerson-Brantingham, he explained, imported from America after the war, had steel wheels and ran on kerosene. You started it with a crank-handle. Its four-cylinder engine was sturdy but the wheels gave a lot of trouble in rough conditions. When wheat prices fell sharply with the Depression, Lawrence found the tractor uneconomical and went back to horses; and then a couple of years ago things began to pick up, so he'd purchased a new German semi-diesel, the Lanz Bulldog. The rubber tyres made it a lot more comfortable, Harry told her. It had no radiator but a hopper instead, using about fifty gallons of water a day to cool the engine. It worked on the lowest grade fuel oil, very cheap. To get it going you had to use a blowtorch on the cylinder.

He talked, too, about the wheat. How the price of it could fluctuate daily. How disease could spoil a good harvest. How the local wheat, Bencubbin, tall and strong, had been regarded as a wonder grain until lately when it became susceptible to a new form of rust. How wheat buyers would insert a metal testing device into a bag to check for diseases such as smut when a load was brought into the Grass Valley siding, but usually did their testing from the bags nearest the scales, so growers liked to load a few bags of smutty wheat on the far side of the truck.

And he told her about some of the farm animals, so well cared for that you'd have thought they were almost members of the family. Nearly human.

'Not just the dogs,' said Harry, 'lovely loyal creatures, the dogs; but the big horses too. Of course we had to look after them very carefully because there was a lot of money invested in them: about twenty-five pounds to buy a sound draught worker of good Clydesdale stock, and you'd need a team of six to pull a plough or harvester. But money aside, it was obvious the Lawrences felt a lot of affection for those horses. It'd take half an hour to bridle and collar the team for farm work, so you got to know them pretty well. And then there was the feeding: same sort of ration four times a day – hay, chaff and oats – and in the stables they'd get rock salt mixed with molasses.

'They were all different, those horses. One of them seemed a bit dull-witted but another one, Toby his name was, big handsome bay, well-flexed hocks with white feathery tufts, had more cunning than three monkeys in a bag. He knew more about farming than I did, that one. He liked to be patted but not all of them did. Some would even try to strike with a front foot when you were putting the collar on. All individuals. A bit like a schoolyard of children, I suppose.

'When I went to work on the farm I heard Tom Lawrence refer sadly to poor Jimmy, and at first I got the impression this was some relative who'd died. But it turned out Jimmy had been a beloved horse. He was one of those big-hearted willing workers who'd keep pulling until he couldn't pull any more, but one day he went into the dam and put his foot through the coupling in the bridle. His head got dragged down and he was drowned. Even though it was months ago, Mr Lawrence is still upset.'

'You've got a gift for describing things, Mr Hopewell,' said Elva. 'The way you use words – it paints a vivid picture of farming out here. Makes me see that life on the land can be really tough.'

Harry nodded. 'Tough? You can say that again. Especially the last few years. A lot of the farmers around this part of the Wheatbelt have been struggling. Now that cars and trucks and tractors are replacing horses, there's not so much fodder farming any more: you can't run a motor engine on hay and chaff. But it's more than that. The land itself isn't as healthy as it should be. A lot of indiscriminate clearing, that's the main problem, you see. The soil's been getting degraded, weed-infested. Soaks and brooks have become salty, many of them. And then of course there've been the constant invasions to cope with.'

'Invasions?' She wrinkled her forehead.

'Marauding animal pests. Hordes of them. It's the drought conditions further inland that have brought them in. Emus everywhere. You can see them high-stepping along the road, squads and squads, as if it's their very own thoroughfare, cheeky devils. Then they get into the paddocks and make a shocking mess of crops. And they can't fly so you can't chase them into the air and away. They just run around, backwards and forwards, waggling their big shaggy mop-like bottoms, stamping everything underfoot and turning it all to dust. A few weeks back, not long before my accident, I was up on the slope behind the sheds trying to shoo away this big emu but it wouldn't take any notice – and then a biplane came out of the clouds and passed fairly close to us, heading for the Northam racecourse I suppose, that's what they've been using for an aerodrome, and the engine noise put the wind up the emu. So it stuck its neck forward and scooted over the hill on its spindly legs, raising little puffs of grey powder as it went. What struck me was the irony of it. Birds are supposed to fly but these ones can't, and humans are supposed to be earthbound but we've built machines that are bigger and faster than anything else in the air.'

Elva laughed appreciatively. The longer he spent talking with her, the more responsive she was to his stories and the more congenial he felt her to be – a kindred spirit, perhaps. Her attention drew words from him fluently.

'Of course the emus aren't the only destructive intruders,' he went on. The bloody rabbits are causing complete havoc, thousands of the buggers. The big government fence line has turned out to be useless, bait only catches small numbers, and Mrs Lawrence won't let anyone use a gun on the farm, not after the terrible tragedy a few years ago.'

'Tragedy?' Elva paused, sponge in hand, eyebrows enquiring.

Harry nodded. 'It'd make a stone weep. Goran told me about it. The eldest of the four Lawrence children were twin boys, really good young fellows, pride of their parents, just sixteen they were, both putting in long hours on the farm, learning all the ropes. You couldn't tell them apart and everyone reckoned they were the best of mates. Tom Lawrence was going to leave the place to them both to share.

'Anyway, this particular day they were up early as usual and headed out to the top paddock with a rifle, after the rabbits. When they didn't come back for the midday meal, and cooees from the farmhouse went unanswered, Tom walked up there looking for them. He found their bodies beside the fence, one lying atop the other. Both had a bullet through the head. It seemed that one of the lads must have accidentally shot his twin when they were climbing through the fence, and then killed himself in a fit of guilty grief.

'It was a shocking thing for the whole district. People could talk of nothing else. They say Tom and his wife have never got over it. And now there's been this accident with the truck, snatching away their other son, young Sammy. The parents will be devastated. It's too much to bear.'

'What do you remember about the crash?'

'Not much. We were on our way back from Northam, Tom driving and Sammy beside him, just sixteen – same age as when his brothers died. I was on the back of the truck, making sure the load of superphosphate bags stayed secure, y'see. We were coming along the home road and as we crested the hill up there I looked over to where Goran was ploughing with the new tractor, and it was so peaceful... the late afternoon light fluttering across in golden ribbons through the roadside trees. And then a big buck kangaroo bounced straight into the side of the cabin with an almighty bang. We swung and skidded. I was flung off the tray like bit of rag, with bags of super toppling around me. I must have been knocked out for a while. When I woke I could hear a lot of moaning, and found it was coming from me. Sammy was already dead. I suppose I drifted off again, because I wasn't conscious of anything else till I found myself in this bed here with bandages and splints all over me.'

As he lay supine for the washing of his private parts, he always watched her and she had avoided eye contact. He wondered whether she could imagine what it was like for him to be touched and not able to touch. He longed to stretch out and put a hand on her while she was leaning over him. But he couldn't even put a hand on himself afterwards to bring some relief.

Each time the routine finished and she walked off down the ward, his eyes followed her slender white-stockinged legs. She was young and embodied vitality; he was about twice her age and a physical wreck. But he couldn't help feeling lascivious – and he doubted that Elva would blame him for it. She was no prude: bodily needs and natural urges were the stuff of her working environment. He could see she was a calmly compassionate person. Anyway, what he felt for her wasn't merely physical. The sharing of their stories had brought a kind of closeness, and he was fairly sure she recognised that.

Fifteen

For the first time since Harry's admission, the matron returned to the ward. He'd heard from Elva that 'the boss' had been convalescing after a bout of gallstone problems. Here she was now, moving slowly from bedside to bedside accompanied by Elva, who gave her an account of each patient's condition and treatment. The matron looked stern, or perhaps just careworn, as she approached Harry.

'So what's the story with this one, nurse?' she asked, jiggling her chatelaine.

'Several broken bones after a road accident,' Elva said, 'and they'll need more time to mend before he can be discharged. As you can see, he's still not able to do anything for himself at the moment. He'll continue to need feeding, washing, and so on, for a month at least.'

'His eye seems to have healed all right, though.'

'Oh, that was an earlier injury.'

As the matron reached for the folder in Elva's hand and opened his file, Harry stared at her face. There was something slightly familiar about her. Then, at the same moment when she suddenly lifted her head from the sheet she was reading, recognition struck him too.

'Harry Hopewell!' she said wonderingly.

'Nellie?' he said. 'Nellie? Is it really you?'

⁓

For weeks he was in a fever of frustration. Neither Elva nor Nellie would exchange more than a few sentences with him. Whenever he tried to talk with Elva she would turn away and busy herself with duties. Whenever he tried to ask Nellie about the lost years she shook her head. 'Not now,' she said firmly.

Though it didn't console him much, he thought he could understand why both women resisted being drawn into conversation with him. Elva's feelings were hurt, no doubt, because the intimacy she'd begun to share with Harry now seemed annulled by the matron's unexplained prior bond with him. Nellie, for her part, probably sensed Elva's curiosity and felt constrained anyway by the proprieties of her own position as matron. Natural enough. For as long as Harry remained bedridden, what else could he expect? Nellie was hardly going to set professional etiquette aside, perch on his bed and start to unlock a personal history that might well contain things difficult to explain.

But he still felt shut out, forlorn. There was no-one else to talk with. The only other patients were a young man with polio, screened off in silent isolation at the far end of the ward, and someone recovering from abdominal surgery who slept most of the time and couldn't make himself understood anyway because of a harelip or some other speech problem.

A month after Harry's accident they removed the splint from his left arm. One of the things he could now do for himself was turn pages. Being able to read again brought welcome distraction – not that there was much choice of reading material. Soon after the accident Mrs Lawrence had brought his scant belongings from the farm to the hospital in a little box. They included a couple of scrapbooks sent to him after his father's death years ago, a string-fastened batch of the lined exercise books he had used as an intermittent diary during the years in Darwin, and the two cherished volumes of Mawson's Antarctic saga.

Pasted into the scrapbooks were miscellaneous items that his father had clipped from newspapers and compiled unsystematically over the years. All the old news cuttings, he recognised, were from the *Herald*, the *Telegraph*, the *Bulletin* or the *Manly Daily*. Some of them were about local events: Taylor's famous gliding flights above the dunes at Narrabeen, the coming of the electric tramline to Collaroy, the controversial auctioning of Salvation Army land, the doubling of the roll at Narrabeen School. Other pieces reflected Bert's attempt to engage with his son's growing interest in wireless: the opening of the Pennant Hills station, the establishment of Amalgamated Wireless Australasia, the first use of wireless sets by the field army in 1916 and by reconnaissance aircraft the next year, the first broadcast from Britain to Australia – Prime Minister Hughes praising troops he had inspected on the Western Front.

Harry turned to the package of his own journals from the war years and spent a couple of hours reading through every entry. Some jottings recorded detachedly his growing awareness that clever inventions would not, after all, be transforming the world as rapidly as he once imagined. *I can see now,* he had written, *that wireless, despite all its promise, probably won't bring any quick changes to the way most people make long-distance contact with one another. For a long while yet, letters are likely to remain the main medium for linking person to person.* Other pages described more about what he had been feeling: distaste for the northern frontier town, impatience with prolonged inaction, acute disappointment as plans dissolved and inertia set in. And the long ache of loneliness. He put his journals aside.

'What a glum bastard you were,' he muttered to himself. *Were?* Are! He'd been in sinking sand for years now.

Mawson's story helped him to fill the silence. Its narrative shape was completely familiar from his previous readings but the details could still absorb him. He wandered now through the chapters, stopping to ruminate when anything caught his attention.

He re-read the passage in which Mawson – his two companions Ninnis and Mertz having died during their dreadful sledding journey across George V Land – returns alone to the base camp to find that the ship has departed but has left behind a small relief group that includes a new wireless operator: Sidney Jeffryes.

Harry began to follow the thread of later references to this young man. Well into the second volume he found particulars that painted a picture of what life down there must have been like for someone on whom the group depended for contact with civilisation. Jeffryes would spend many hours every night listening for messages and calling at short intervals while also making notes of the intensity of the signals and of atmospheric interference from static discharges or snow particles or auroral activity. Harry imagined him bent over the wireless receiver, nerves taut as he tried for long periods to shut out all the noisy distractions: the wind roaring outside, ordinary sounds within the hut, the barking of dogs in their veranda shelter, and occasionally thunder or the crackle of St Elmo's fire.

Winds, so relentless that they almost seemed to rip through Mawson's pages, often made the wire stays of the mast go slack, and Jeffryes needed continually to pull them taut on his daily maintenance patrols. Once, violent gusts had hurled him to the ground, bruising his ribs.

Then, in mid-1913, according to Mawson, 'Jeffryes became ill, and for some weeks his symptoms were such as to give everyone much anxiety'. His problem worsened: 'the continual and acute strain of sending and receiving messages under unprecedented conditions was such that he eventually had a nervous breakdown'. And that was all except for a reticent comment in an appendix, referring to 'the illness of Mr S. N. Jeffryes, who took up so conscientiously the duties of wireless operator during the second year, but upon whom the monotony of a troglodytic winter life made itself felt'. A footnote recorded that Jeffryes had suffered a relapse upon his return to Australia.

Putting the book aside, Harry sank into a moody meditation. He could almost feel the intolerable weight of a polar wilderness pressing on his mind, and believed he could understand how the intense frustrations of trying to reach out by wireless to the wide world from that terrible place had driven Sidney Jeffryes into madness. Yet he knew that other members of the expedition faced even more atrocious circumstances while handling similar duties calmly. Walter Hannam, the operator who preceded Jeffryes at the Cape Denison base, had remained in cheerful spirits despite being unable to make any reliable wireless contact. His small party of colleagues on Macquarie Island were continually buffeted by gales as they struggled to haul the generator and other huge loads up a steep hill and erect the masts and huts there, and then had to wait many months before they succeeded in relaying messages to and from Antarctica, but proved during their two years of isolation to be an ingenious and resilient band even when their food supplies dwindled almost to nothing. What caused one man to lose his nerve while others showed unshakeable fortitude? Invoking 'character' did little to explain the difference.

Keen to discuss this conundrum, he tried raising it with Nellie when she stopped beside his bed one evening. But she brushed the matter aside before he could say much about it. 'I can't linger, Harry,' she said. 'This isn't the time or place for exchanging deep thoughts.'

A sudden commotion woke him before dawn one morning. Shouts were erupting shapelessly into the ward. In the dim light Harry could see that the man with the harelip had climbed out of bed. He was gesticulating like a madman as his inarticulate noise battered the air. A young nurse assistant cowered near him and sobbed like a schoolgirl.

'Hey!' Harry called out. 'What's all this about?'

The nurse evaded the patient's flailing arms and ran to press an alarm button on the wall before scuttling over to Harry's bedside.

'What's happened?' Harry asked her.

'He's got into this rage,' she wailed, 'just because I said I couldn't understand what he was trying to tell me. He won't stop yelling.'

The man stumbled towards them, still bellowing, his face livid and distorted. There was a big patch of blood on the front of his pyjama jacket. He shook his finger at the whimpering nurse. Harry, immobile, could do nothing to restrain or calm him.

Then Elva came quickly into the ward, wrapping her flannel dressing-gown around her. Sizing up the situation in a moment, she strode over to the man.

'That's enough, Mr Alcorn,' she said resolutely, with a firm hand on his shoulder. 'You come with me. Yes, this way. Let's get you back into your bed and we'll have a look at that wound. It seems to have opened up. Come on now. Shush – just lie still.' The patient obeyed her meekly.

A strong current of emotion jolted Harry's body. The way Elva had dealt with the emergency – calm, decisive, authoritative – made him want to applaud. And touch her, too. There was a quality in her physical presence that aroused not only his admiration but also a yearning for contact. It was a strange, untroubled bond that they had forged – broken unwittingly by the re-entry into his life of another woman, one who had once seemed all in all to him but was now a stranger.

And at that moment there she was, this spectre from the past: Nellie, in full Matron's regalia, had just arrived at the door of the ward where she stood looking somehow indecisive and ineffectual as Elva was carefully wiping blood from around the wound of the man she had pacified.

⌒

When at last the time arrived for Harry's discharge, Nellie came to him.

'We can release you now from hospital,' she said, 'but you'll need to be careful and build up your strength before you can think of working again. No question of being able to return to farm work or anything like that. So where are you going to go?'

'Don't know. Don't seem to have any options.'

'Well, the Matron's house is next door to here and there's a spare room. I suggest you stay with me till you get back on your feet.'

He could only indicate his thanks with a nod, feeling foolishly passive and inarticulate.

Sixteen

'It was the evening of that concert in the zoo gardens,' she began, stirring the sugar slowly into her teacup. 'At the last minute you couldn't go with me – remember?'

More than a quarter of a century ago now, but of course he remembered that disappointment.

'Certainly do. I'd come down with an aching fever the night before. Throat so raw I could hardly talk, nose streaming, eyes sore and swollen. So I sent you the tickets with an apologetic note, asking you to take young Doris with you.'

He didn't mention, but recalled with painful clarity, his sharp chagrin when he later found by chance that Nellie had gone there without Doris Biddle; and recalled, too, her irritable reaction when he reproved her for not telling him.

'Well,' she went on after taking a slow deep breath, fingertips pressed to her temple, 'something happened to me that night, something dreadful. The concert was pleasant enough, except that I felt awkward being there on my own.

I'd have enjoyed the skills of the musicians more if you'd been sitting there with me, Harry. And the romantic atmosphere – the coloured lights, the fountains – all lovely, but I was almost the only person in the audience who wasn't part of a couple or a group. So I began to think it was foolish of me to go unaccompanied. When you had to withdraw, and then Doris too, my thought was, you see, that by attending alone I could give you an account of the concert later. I didn't want you to miss even a second-hand experience, after you'd been so nice as to buy the tickets. But that was naive of me. How could I have described the music and the festivity? I don't have the right words for things like that. And anyway, as it turned out, the pleasantness was spoiled, obliterated, by what occurred after the concert.' She fidgeted with her teaspoon, and ran the tip of her tongue over her teeth.

'I was making my way towards the exit when someone spoke to me. It was Mr Riven. All the details are still in my head; I'll never forget them. "Good evening, Miss Weston," he said. "You're not here without a companion, surely?" I admitted I was, and he told me firmly he wouldn't let me walk home unescorted. It was a moonless night, and although our bakery wasn't very far off I did feel apprehensive at the prospect of making my solitary way along those dark streets. He said he had to wait a few minutes for the crowds to leave and then it was his responsibility to extinguish the lights and lock the gates – after which he'd see me safely to my doorstep.

'The Rivens were family friends, you know; we saw them every Sunday at our chapel. So it didn't cross my mind that I was putting myself in any danger. But I suppose you can guess what I'm leading up to. As soon as the lights were out he seized me from behind in a tight embrace and put a hand up under my dress. When I struggled he forced me down on to the grass and held a handkerchief over my mouth while he pulled roughly at my clothes with his other hand, grunting and snuffling like a pig. Even now, bringing it all back to mind makes me sick and angry. It was disgusting, a horrible ordeal. I felt so degraded. After it was all over and he let me go, I ran home along the dark streets, sobbing.'

Her voice and hands had begun to shake. Harry, shocked, began to murmur something intended to calm her, but she brushed his words aside, frowning.

'No – let me tell all of it.' She blew her nose noisily, and sipped her tea. 'Everything's been pent up so long, and then even when you turned up miraculously in my little hospital and we found each other, I couldn't start recounting any of this because there were nurses around and busy things I needed to keep doing as matron, so I've had to wait all this time until you could be discharged and sit down here quietly with me.

'My parents…' She stopped, pressing her lips together tightly and twisting her handkerchief this way and that.

'My parents had waited up for me, and…of course they could see at once that something had happened, something very nasty. There were filthy stains on my dress, and my eyes must have been puffy with tears. My father leapt to his feet in an instant rage – you know what he was like, Harry, so you can imagine the scene. He was shouting your name but I insisted you weren't to blame in any way and knew nothing of my plight, hadn't been able to escort me after all, being ill; and it was of my own accord that I'd gone to the zoo alone.'

'He must have been furious when you told him who was responsible.'

Nellie shook her head. 'Furious he was, yes – but as for the responsibility, it just didn't come out like that, you see, because I told an impulsive lie. I'm not sure why, really. Out of some strange sort of shame, I suppose, that I'd put myself in such a vulnerable position. And perhaps out of a sense that my parents would hardly be able to believe that Riven, a member of our own church fellowship, had done this, violating me, and violating my family's friendship too. Anyhow, I just said I'd been attacked in the street on the way home and I had no idea who'd done it.'

Harry put a hand across his mouth as if to stop himself from expostulating. Nellie had paused and seemed momentarily to have slipped into a trance. Then she blinked, sucked in a deep sighing breath and continued her story.

'My father strode up and down the passage, and past the doorway of the room where my mother and I sat weeping. He just muttered and made a kind of hissing sound. Not a single word of comfort. He was like a bear in a cage. I remember seeing the fleck of foam at the corner of his mouth. Eventually he stopped in front of me, glared, and said to my mother, "Get her into a bath. Neither of you will say anything about this to anyone. And we are NOT going to talk about it. Not to each other. Not to anyone else. Not at all. Never!"

'But much later, about three months, when there could be no doubt I was carrying a child, my mother had to tell him about my condition, and he went livid – shouted something vile, slammed the door on us, rushed fuming into the street, and didn't come back for an hour or more. On his return he announced – I can hear him now, his tone all cold and hard – that we'd be leaving town quietly that night and must pack a small bag each, straight away, only a few essential things, nothing more. We wouldn't ever be returning to the bakery. He didn't let us discuss anything, or say a word to anybody.'

'If only I'd known...'

'He was adamant that no-one could be told we were going, let alone where. And so we left, about midnight it was, and kept trudging through the small hours along to the causeway and then right on up to the rail station. We huddled in the waiting room there for part of the morning and later we caught the first train south and got off at Bunbury – why he decided that was the place to stop I don't know.'

'And you stayed in Bunbury?'

'Well, he found cheap board for Mum and me immediately with a spinster, Mrs Prebble, a prune-faced crabby old thing she was, too. She soon guessed my condition – I was vomiting a lot with the morning sickness by this time – and she made it clear from her expression and tone of voice that she had a low opinion of me for being pregnant as a single woman. But I suppose we were lucky to have a roof over our heads. We lived uneasily in her house for a long while, staying on after the baby was born.'

'What did you do for money?'

'My dad got work timber-cutting at Wellington Mills, so he only saw us every Sunday when he came in on the train from Dardanup. To be frank, I think he was glad to be living in a different house from me, and I can't say I was sorry about being apart from him during the week. In his eyes, what had happened was all my own fault, and he didn't want much to do with me. I think he'd have liked to hide me away completely if he could. Each Sunday he'd go off with Mum to church – it was the Baptists now; he cut us off completely from the

Methodists – but I always had to stay behind at Mrs Prebble's, and I doubt he'd have mentioned my existence to anyone.

'When the time came for my confinement, he arranged for me to move into a discreet little hostel run by nuns. Very stern and spartan. Straight after the birth I was indescribably tired – they must have given me something to knock me out – and when eventually I woke up they wouldn't bring the baby to me, wouldn't let me hold her or see her at all. They just told me she would be going to a good home and be well looked after. That was all I could get out of them, except that one young nun took pity on me later as I sobbed my heart out: she whispered to me that my baby was a healthy, pretty, red-haired little girl – but no, there was no way I'd ever be able to discover her adoptive name or track her down. And I never could. I've no idea where she is or what became of her. This is the first time for many years that I've spoken of her.'

Nellie stopped talking, picked up the teapot and went into the kitchen. Mouth ajar, Harry stared out the window, seeing nothing.

The kettle whistled. Nellie brought the freshened pot back to the table in its crocheted cosy and poured cups for them both. She dabbed at her eyes with the corner of her apron. They sipped at their tea in silence, not looking at each other.

In the days that followed he heard more of her story, conveyed piecemeal between her stints of hospital duty. Having disburdened herself of her painful secret, Nellie spoke more freely about things that had happened after her baby disappeared into the anonymous fog of adoption.

She had moved, she said, to the little Wheatbelt town of Tammin with her parents, who took out a lease on vacant tearooms that had modest living quarters upstairs. Nellie helped to serve the customers. It was a scraping sort of existence for the first few months but they were thrifty and contrived to make ends meet. The couple next door befriended them: Norman Higgs was in retirement after a long prosperous career as manager of the Tammin branch of the Agricultural Bank, and his wife Hettie was still a driving force in the local Country Women's Association. They had a cream Buick Century convertible coupé, which Norm polished religiously and which was the envy of everyone in town. Very seldom did anyone else get to ride in it; so it was a mark of social approval when, a year after moving to Tammin, Mr and Mrs Weston were invited by their neighbours to come for a drive while Nellie was minding the shop. The gleaming machine took them on a tour around the town, up to see Yorkrakine Rock, back again, then straight into the path of a fast-moving sheep-wagon train at the Tammin rail crossing. All four occupants of the Buick died instantly, and a welter of maimed mutton littered the track.

As soon as her parents were buried, Nellie moved to Northam in search of work. Her timing was lucky: there was an opening for a junior nurse assistant at the hospital.

'It took me a fair while to learn the ropes,' she told Harry, resting her hand against the warmth of the tea cosy. 'The effort of trying to ignore how unhappy I was made me tired, deeply tired, and there's a lot to nursing that's unpleasant anyway. It's not all starched cuffs and collar, you know. We've never had enough funds for all the equipment we'd like, and especially during the worst of the Depression we just had to shrug and make do. Using kerosene tins and Primus stoves to sterilise things, for example. Anyhow, over the years I picked up a fair bit of experience and eventually when the matron retired I got the job. So here I am now.'

'Enjoy the work?'

'Wouldn't say enjoy. It's just been something to do, that's all. It's kept the mind off…'

She took a gingernut biscuit from the tin and dunked it in her tea. That frown again, that gnawing of the lip.

'What I mean is,' she went on, 'it's helped me to face being on my own all these years. Not exactly a cheerful life, to be frank, and I'd be dwelling too much on that if I didn't have a busy job.'

'Never thought of marriage?'

Nellie sniffed and cleared her throat. 'Used to think about it half my waking hours. But the thoughts always led back to you, Harry, and I'd start feeling sorry for myself all over again. It was like a miserable little refrain going round and round in my head: if only you hadn't got sick that time, everything could have worked out perfectly for us. Couldn't it? We were so happy in each other's company, weren't we? We'd have got engaged before long, surely. But then everything changed, and afterwards I felt ashamed and hopeless. All those years went by, wasted years. After my mum and dad died and I came to Northam, it did cross my mind to try to find out where you were. Perhaps get in touch somehow. But where would I have started looking? I couldn't face returning to South Perth, having to answer questions from people I'd known, perhaps coming face to face with Riven. Anyway I thought you'd probably gone back to Sydney – might as well have been on the moon. And what would've been the point of tracking you down? I'd have needed to tell you what had happened, and that would've been the end of it. End of the dream. I didn't dare imagine that you'd remain unmarried, just like me.'

She gave a rueful watery smile that wavered into resignation. Neither looked at the other. Their sadness stretched out wordlessly between them. Harry could not think of anything to say.

Nellie glanced at the mantelpiece clock. 'I'll have to be back on duty in half an hour. But I've done all the talking these past few days, Harry. You haven't told me much about how you've spent your time all these years. How things worked out for you.'

'Not too well, obviously. That's the short version. I'll tell you more another time.'

'All right, the details can wait. But meantime don't keep me completely in the dark. Those aspirations, the things you were so intent on doing and used to talk about with such enthusiasm, like piloting an aeroplane – did you get to do any of that?'

'Flying? Nup. Didn't happen. The cards never fell my way.'

He told her briefly about the dead ends and lost horizons.

'So what are you going to do with yourself, now you're out of hospital?'

'What can I do, Nellie? My right arm's bloody near useless. I'm blind in one eye.'

She fiddled with her teaspoon, put it down, picked it up again and tapped it against her chin.

'You can live here with me,' she said at last, quietly, 'if you want to. Permanently. Together, I mean – as a couple. Hasn't that crossed your mind? Getting married after all?'

'But I'm not the man I used to be. You wouldn't want to tie yourself to a deadbeat. Marrying isn't something to do out of pity.'

'It's not pity I'm feeling, you silly galoot.'

⌒

'Are you quite sure you don't want a more elaborate ceremony?' he had asked.

'No point,' she said with a shrug. 'Neither of us has any family or special friends to invite.'

So their wedding was as perfunctory as the law allowed, and he kept to himself the nagging awareness that had haunted him for weeks.

The more he thought about Nellie's story, the more likely it seemed that her kinfolk were known to him. All the details could fit. The Ruth he knew so well might be – must be, he had begun to believe – Nellie's lost child: she was just the right age, had vivid red hair and pale skin, with eyes the same colour as Nellie's, grew up in Bunbury, and had no definite information about her parentage.

But he also saw at once that he could never reveal to Nellie what he suspected about her daughter's identity; nor could he ever tell Ruth about Nellie. It was impossible to divulge any of this to anybody because of the devastating probability that Ruth had unwittingly married the son of her mother's violator. If Patrick was indeed Ruth's half-brother, then their daughter – Nellie's granddaughter – was the fruit of an incestuous union. Harry knew he must conceal this cruel truth as his own painful secret, hidden away behind his ribs, or it would bring terrible grief not only to Nellie but also to the little family.

Seventeen

His clumsiness vexed him. Having to use his left hand to heft a small axe with a sawn-off handle so that he could chop blocks of wood for the stove made him feel feeble, off balance. But the other hand still lacked the strength for gripping anything tightly, probably always would, and anyway there wasn't much flexibility in that arm. The fingers of his right hand curled stiffly. He thought it looked like a dog's paw, and he kept it in his pocket whenever possible.

Washing clothes, too – it was awkward to hold them in place with his gammy hand against the corrugated scrubbing board as he clenched the soap and rubbed at the stains; then he'd have to poke them down with a stick into the copper for the boil-up, lift them out for a cold-water rinse in the tub, put them through the ringer while turning the handle, and at last peg out each piece laboriously on the clothesline and raise it with the prop. All with only one useful hand. Other tasks posed the same problem. Cutting up food to prepare meals was a slow and tedious business. Even drying the dishes took longer than it should.

He didn't much mind picking up a woman's work, though it did feel a bit strange each morning when she left for the hospital and he turned again to the household chores. Well, no point in feeling sorry for himself. It would be a long time before he could hold down a paid job, if ever. His injuries restricted him too much. To show that he saw the funny side of it, he opened the door to her one evening wearing her frilly apron, knotted headscarf and slippers. She shrieked with laughter.

Joking aside, he could see that Nellie was comfortable with the arrangement.

'I may as well continue as matron,' she had said with a shrug. 'I'm used to it. Probably wouldn't know what to do with myself if I stopped. Anyway, the wages are good enough to cover our needs.'

'I suppose there's something apt about a baker's daughter turning out to be a breadwinner,' he said wryly.

'Have to be realistic, Harry. There's not a lot you can do right now except make yourself useful looking after the house and vegie garden, getting supplies from the shops, that sort of thing. If your arm gets better, we can start thinking about how to organise things differently.'

But they knew it wouldn't get better.

Her job was no sinecure. The scheduled hours were long and she had to be available when called on outside those hours. It was also her responsibility to keep a weather eye on the nursing quarters behind the Matron's house. Closing the door firmly on the day's troubles wasn't possible. Often, over a cup of tea after the evening meal, she talked about some of her hospital patients, past and present. This, he could see, was her way of trying to siphon the piteous images out of her head – images of people cruelly struck down, wasted by disease, by madness, by many kinds of suffering. He knew when she was feeling agitated, whether by something she had just witnessed or by scenes recalled from an earlier time. She would stir the sugar noisily into her tea, tap tap tap with the spoon against the outside of the cup, and twist the spoon around as she stared at it. Then she would blurt something: 'Young Peter Banks let out a terrible scream this morning, took a fit and went into a coma by the time the nurse reached him – probably won't come out of it,' or, 'I've been thinking all day of a little lass called Violet Sheridan, diphtheria, choked to death in front of us a couple of years ago,' or, 'That poor sod Bert Ingram kept vomiting and soiling himself through the night. Blood, too, both ends. We can't get the smell out of the ward. Had to move him to the veranda.'

Harry would sit quietly, nodding now and then, until she had got everything off her chest. Then he would put his good arm around her shoulder to help her calm down.

The listening wasn't all one-sided. He sometimes needed a sympathetic ear too. There was a lot to tell Nellie about his own troubles, a lot to explain. He wanted her to know what a long run of bad luck he'd had. He wanted her to understand how it wasn't for lack of ability or effort that his plans and hopes had come to nothing.

'Let's face it, Nellie,' he said one evening, 'most of my adult life has been a series of heavy setbacks, and I can't pretend to have the patience of Job.'

'Look, I don't blame you for feeling down in the dumps,' she replied. 'Still, you must try to pull yourself together. If you keep sliding into self-pity it makes everything harder for us both.'

'The fact is, though, I've achieved nothing of what I wanted to do.'

'But you shouldn't see that as a personal failure, Harry. You could say it's the modern world that has failed *you*. It hasn't turned out the way you'd hoped.'

He was silent for a while before saying, 'I remember a line from a poem we learnt at school: "'Tis not too late to seek a newer world" – but it really *is* too late, I'm afraid. For me, anyway.'

There was little they could do together in Northam. They went occasionally to the Capitol Cinema, where a few films plucked at their feelings. Harry was so impressed by *The Broken Melody* that he sat through it a second time. To watch and hear Australian characters on the screen, taking part in a serious drama filmed by Cinesound and set partly in Sydney during the Depression years, enacting failure and recovery – he found that absorbing. Some of the scenes and snatches of conversation stayed with him. 'Optimism wears out with your boots,' he repeated to himself.

They saw Katherine Hepburn and Cary Grant in *Bringing Up Baby*. Amusing, Harry thought, that 'Baby' turned out to be Hepburn's tame leopard. Nellie and he both laughed when Hepburn sang, 'I Can't Give You Anything But Love, Baby', but Harry wondered if they were laughing for the same reason. The part where Baby got mistaken for a vicious leopard escaped from a circus made him recall the day he and Nellie had spent at the zoo. There was something familiar, too, about the way the leopard yawned, and it came to the front of his mind as they walked home from the cinema: the little grey cat in Weston's bakery years ago.

'Hey!' He turned towards Nellie and put a hand on her elbow. 'Remember your old mouser – Beastly?'

'Now that you mention her, yes. It's ages since I gave her a thought. But I did feel a lot of affection for Beastly when I was a child and she was still a kitten. She had to endure being given speech lessons by me. Yes, ridiculous, I know. I wanted her at least to recognise a few words. She wasn't an apt pupil, but that was the nearest I got to glimpsing what it might be like to have an infant sister. Leaving her behind when we… Well, that was very hard. I hope someone looked after her.'

'I can set your mind at rest. She certainly didn't go short of a meal or a bit of companionship. Attached herself pretty quickly to the Biddles next door.'

'The little traitor! She should have been inconsolable.'

'Cats are good at consoling themselves.'

After their evening meal, Harry would usually spend the time reading while Nellie updated the entries in her hospital log.

'Same old book, eh?' she said, smiling to show that she didn't mean it unkindly. 'That Antarctic story. So what is it that holds your interest?'

He looked up, marking the place with his finger, and pondered the question.

'These blokes weren't just brave,' he said. 'They were brainy too. They adapted whatever was at hand to the requirements of the moment. I mean, picture Mawson himself – I've just been re-reading this bit: there he is, struggling back towards his base across those vast stretches of ice, and he needs a substitute for the crampons discarded earlier on his journey, so he cuts two pieces of wood from a theodolite box, sticks into them as many screws and tacks as he can prise from the sledge, and sets off with the pieces of studded wood lashed underneath his feet!'

Harry shook his head in admiration, and went on: 'They came up with all sorts of other quick-witted little inventions, too. How do you like this, for instance? There were a couple of groups building the wireless relay station on Macquarie Island, you see, and they had to communicate with each other in a howling wind while one group was at the base of a hill and the other at the top, so they made themselves heard by shouting through megaphones they'd shaped from an old pair of leggings. Great improvisers, those fellows. There are lots of other examples. A windproof lantern, things like that.'

He could see she wasn't much impressed.

'But they were facing exceptional challenges, weren't they?' she said. 'The situation was really extreme for them. Doesn't have much to do with the struggles of ordinary people here and now.'

Harry didn't respond. But I didn't ever want to be ordinary, said the voice in his head.

Silence settled on them. They might as well have been sitting in separate rooms. He put the book aside. After a few minutes he went to the back door and stood there sucking on a cigarette. When it was finished he flicked the butt out into the darkness and watched its red tip somersault through a fading arc.

Living in the Matron's house next door to the little hospital could hardly have been more convenient, but he was beginning to feel uneasy. The yearning that had persisted through those long years of separation should have transformed itself now into a climax of fulfilment. Yet it wasn't turning out like that, after all. The home they were trying to make together hadn't become a blissful one, though he doubted that Nellie thought much about this. She seemed to be taking it for granted that their shared life was something he wanted, that he found it satisfying, that the feelings he had expressed so many years ago remained intact. Or perhaps, with his prospects debilitated by misfortune, she just assumed he was in no position to aspire to anything more than this. Probably she saw him as having become passive, inert, and he couldn't deny it was so. He wondered, too, whether his disfigured eye-socket repelled her. If it did, he could hardly hold that against her. Every time she looked at him she must be aware of the contrast between his battered body and the youthful figure he'd cut when she first met him.

But did she understand, conversely, that the Nellie he'd found was not the Nellie he'd once lost? That the woman so long desired was irretrievable? While the years had treated him harshly, they had not left unmarked this person with whom he now shared house and bed. Her dentures had spoilt the smile she used to have. Her hair looked lank, her once creamy skin had started to go mottled, and in the mornings her breath was sometimes stale. There was a time when her voice had delighted him, but now, when she spoke, her voice often seemed to grate like one sheet of corrugated iron rubbing against another on a windy night.

Yet there was nothing cold in what he felt towards her; rather, loyalty mingled with compassion. Her need for these things was like blotting paper, he thought. Or like sandy soil, thirstily soaking up his spirit. Was she moved by any deep tenderness for him? He could not detect it. Nevertheless he did his best to be companionable. And he should try harder, he told himself, to lift their mood, to reach for the liveliness that had electrified their youthful conversations.

Her flesh did not befriend him as he had once thought it would. When they first approached one another's bodies it was tentatively, like shy animals. Their couplings became wordless and ravenous, taking them together to a crest of urgency; but each time they finished and fell back on the bed, he sensed they were more apart than ever, and he noticed she often seemed on the verge of shedding a tear at that moment. Intimate strangers.

Sometimes Harry liked to take a leisurely walk along O'Connor's pipeline to the construction work that was going ahead steadily at the Army Camp on the town common. Mess huts and building materials from the old training ground at Blackboy Hill were being relocated to this Northam camp. According to the talk in town, it would be the permanent western headquarters for troop training. It seemed pretty clear that the army was preparing seriously for war.

Apart from that, Northam was a sleepy place. The farming families didn't mix much with the townsfolk. The railway workers generally kept to themselves at one end of the town and the commercial people clustered at the other end. Harry found it difficult to strike up much of a conversation except with Wally Duff, the local tobacconist and chief chatterbox. It was from Wally that he picked up gossip about the Army

Camp, rumours about the Shire Council officers, and miscellaneous scraps of information about the town's social boundaries.

'I never see any blackfellas around here,' he said to Wally.

'You'd have seen plenty here until a few years ago,' Wally declared, thumbs hooked into his braces as he tipped his weight gently to and fro, heel to toe. 'Six or seven years, it must be. The Shire Council thought they were a health risk – scabies was the main worry, and we'd had a couple of bad cases in the hospital – so the police rounded them up like animals, removed the whole Aboriginal population of Northam and took them to the Moore River Settlement.'

Harry thought he could imagine something of what those blackfellas would have felt. He knew a bit about displacement himself.

At home the wireless gave him the illusion of company. Harry usually kept it turned on for most of the day. The town's own radio broadcaster, 6AM Northam, called itself The Happy Station, and some of its programs were relayed from 6PM Perth, which declared itself to be The Cheery Station. Happy? Cheery? Only for those whose spirits were easy to lift, whose glad-heartedness sat near the surface. The songs that the station played repeatedly were trite but he couldn't stop the tunes and words from tinkling in his head: 'Pocket full of Dreams', 'Whistle While You Work', 'Over the Rainbow'. Silly sentiments that had nothing to do with the life he was living or the social and political realities around him.

The local member of parliament, young Bert Hawke the Labor man, had been re-elected earlier in the year but most of the townspeople didn't seem to think it mattered much who was running the state. The fact that the country had emerged slowly from the big Depression could hardly be attributed to any government policy. And in Harry's eyes there still wasn't a lot to be cheery about, anyway. The news reports from Europe had been worrying him for a long while, and now every time he opened the paper or watched a newsreel at the Capitol or listened to a BBC report through the local station it seemed that the international outlook was getting gloomier.

'Germany's still doing whatever it likes,' he said to Nellie one evening. 'Italy, too. The League of Nations doesn't have the guts to stand up to them. It's been like this for two or three years, or more. Remember reading about Haile Selassie's appeal to the League? Eloquent, but it didn't stop Italy from occupying Ethiopia with impunity. Didn't stop Mussolini's army from using mustard gas. Disgusting. The way things are going, there'll be war right across Europe and Africa before long. It'll spread, too. I bet Australia'll be drawn yet again into quarrels between other nations. It's going to be another bloody disaster.'

⌣

'Lovely morning, Mr Fricker,' Harry called out across the fence, trying to sound more optimistic than he felt.

The whiskery old man kneeling beside a row of lettuces looked up at him askance.

'What's lovely about it?' he sniffed. Tufts of hair made a snowy frame for large rubicund ears.

'Well, let's see – the weather, for a start. Not a single cloud in the sky. Warm but not too warm, eh? And look at your vegetables – you must be pleased at the way they're thriving.'

Arnold Fricker gave him a baleful glare.

'Don't go thinking you can help yourself to any of them,' he warned.

'No need to worry,' said Harry soothingly, accustomed to this kind of irrational mistrust from his elderly neighbour. 'We've got our own crop here.'

Fricker stuck out his lower lip like a pouting child and turned back silently to his weeding. It was this way whenever Harry tried to engage him in conversation.

'What's up with old Fricker next door?' Harry had asked Nellie. 'He always seems hostile. Likes picking arguments.'

'It's nothing you've done,' she replied. 'He's like that with anyone. Senile. Mad as a cut snake. Started to go cranky a few years back, during the Depression. Seems it was Throssell's death that set him off. Hugo Throssell – that writer's husband. They called him Jim around here. I suppose you know about his suicide?'

'Matter of fact, I do, yes. But why would that affect old Arnold Fricker?'

'Well, Throssell was a Northam boy, prominent family, and what I heard was that Fricker's son had been a mate of Throssell's here, and they joined the 10th Light Horse together and went off to Gallipoli. But young Fricker was killed over there – same action that got Throssell his Victoria Cross. Anyway, Throssell wrote a letter of condolence, and kept in touch after the war. Old Arnold had a high regard for Throssell and saw him as almost like a son – filling the hole in his life that his own boy had left. So when Throssell died the way he did, it was like that first bereavement all over again.'

'Poor beggar.'

After a ruminative pause, Nellie spoke again. 'Heroism – it's a strange thing, isn't it? A man can be amazingly brave in the heat of battle, protecting and encouraging his men, making light of his wounds, picking up bombs and throwing them back at the Turks, holding his ground in the face of frightening odds. But a few years later, in peacetime, he sits on his veranda and turns his gun on himself.'

'There's something else, too,' Harry added. 'It's ironical, really, that Throssell was a genuine Australian war hero.'

'Why ironical?'

'Look at his name.'

'What do you mean?'

'Throssell. German origin, isn't it? So is Hugo. I bet his forebears came from the Fatherland. Anyway it's a reminder that there's something random about national identity. I used to know someone who was left holding the unlucky end of the same stick – Max Schank, I worked with him on the Applecross wireless station. He'd lived in Australia for years, no less loyal to our country than the next man, but because he came from Germany they locked him up during the war like a zoo animal, and packed him off to Europe when it ended.'

A few days later, Harry was woken by the sound of sticks being thrown at their bedroom window. When he pulled up the blind and looked out, he saw Arnold Fricker peering over the fence and glaring at him. Harry went outside in his pyjamas and remonstrated.

'Hey! No need for that, Mr Fricker,' he called out. 'What's the matter, eh?'

'Know about Captain Jim Throssell, do you?' said Fricker.

'Yes, very sad, his suicide.'

'It was no suicide. They said he shot himself, but that's a lie. Killed by the bloody government. That's who did it.'

'Why would they do a thing like that, Mr Fricker?'

'Because Jim and his wife were spreading socialist ideas, of course!'

'Come off it. You're barking up the wrong tree. Our system's based on freedom of speech. Anyway, what's it got to do with us? Why are you throwing things at our window?'

'Because,' Fricker shouted, 'you're working for the government!'

'Eh? I'm out of work – you know that.'

'Can't fool me,' said Fricker, wagging an admonitory finger. 'I know what you're up to. You told me yourself you used to build wireless transmitters. Don't think I haven't worked out why. It's so the government can put messages into my head. Sending out those invisible rays into everybody's home. Try to control the whole population. Well, they won't get me. Just you watch this!'

The old man lifted up a compact Bakelite radio set so that Harry could see it, and then carried it to a corner of his yard, set it on a chopping block and smashed it to pieces with an axe.

'Got something here for you, Mr Hopewell. Just a mo. Poste restante.' The postmistress reached into a drawer, beamed at him and held out an envelope as if proffering a personally chosen gift.

'Thanks, Mrs Bunting.' Harry squinted at it, postmarked in Perth and addressed in a hand he didn't recognise: Mr Harold Hopewell, c/- Post Office, Northam.

Lifting the flap with his finger, he pulled out the letter and then sat in the sun on a low stone wall outside the church nearby to read it. It was from someone called George Lawson, in Port Kembla, New South Wales, declaring himself 'a relative' who wanted to make contact.

That evening Harry told Nellie about the letter, reading bits of it to her.

'Says here he came over to the west to trace me, and his enquiries took him to South Perth, where someone at the Windsor Hotel told him I'd moved up near Northam. Then he goes on, "Should this letter reach you, please reply to the address above and let me know where I can find you. If you're in or around Northam I'd like to visit you there. I have some family information that will be of interest, but I want to convey it in person." What do you make of that? Why would he want to come all the way here to look me up?' Harry shook his head and shrugged. 'D'you reckon I might be getting a big inheritance from some unknown wealthy cousin, eh?' He chuckled to show he wasn't serious.

He sent a reply inviting Lawson to come and stay for a few days. One afternoon less than a fortnight later, a few days after war had been declared, there was a knock at the door. Harry opened it to find a tall lean man standing there, someone whose smooth, tinted skin and unusual eyes made it hard for Harry to guess his age. The visitor could have been younger or older than himself. His features were distinctively Chinese.

'Very pleased to meet you, Mr Hopewell,' said this man in perfect English as he held out his hand to clasp Harry's bent paw. 'I'm George Lawson. Despite appearances and names, we're closely related.'

Eighteen

It was an astonishing tale that George Lawson related over their evening meal.

'Hard to decide where to begin,' he said. 'You'll want to know how I became aware of our family connection, but I can't explain that without telling you a bit about my background for a start. I wouldn't have got hold of the full story myself if it hadn't been for your Aunt Muriel. She tracked me down a couple of years back, and it took a fair bit of persistence on her part. Last she'd heard of me I was still a boy, boarding in Goulburn. St Patrick's College – the Christian Brothers school. A rough place in some ways, but I wasn't the only half-breed boy there and we soon learned to shrug at the name-calling. Team sport was a big thing at St Pat's, especially rugby. I enjoyed the game a lot, played out on the wing and did pretty well though I say so myself, quite speedy, so after a while that earned me a certain amount of grudging acceptance. In my last year there the coach said, "You may not be the best winger in the school, Lawson, but for a Chinaman you're not bad." I studied hard too. Got a prize for English expression – amusing, eh?'

Harry smiled politely, suppressing an impulse to ask their visitor to get to the point. Reminiscence about school days from someone they'd just met seemed self-indulgent.

'Anyway,' Lawson continued, 'that school gave me a decent start in life. I count myself lucky. When I left it wasn't easy to find a job of any kind, but the fact I'd been to St Pat's opened a door eventually. One of the Brothers wrote a letter of introduction for me to take to a man who'd been to the same school in its early days. He was running a newspaper in Bowral, *The Wollondilly Press*, and wanted an office boy who could set type and do odd jobs, so I spent several years there. It was a good honest little country paper, circulating in Moss Vale, Mittagong, Berrima, and a few other places. We were proud of it. Well, the war came along and I enlisted, and off I went to Gallipoli and then the Western Front, picked up some nasty shrapnel in my shoulder and spent a while in an English hospital.'

Harry's mouth twitched impatiently. Where was this story going? He wanted Lawson to get on with explaining the family connection he claimed to have. What did he mean by saying Aunt Muriel knew about him when he was a boy? But Nellie was keen to hear more of the man's wartime experiences.

'How can you pass over those things so lightly?' she said. 'The fighting, I mean, and getting wounded, and all that. I've never heard a soldier describe what it was really like to be in the thick of it.'

Their Chinese visitor shook his head. 'That's because most of what we suffered in the trenches was far too dreadful to talk about. You just can't imagine… Mud and blood oozing all around us, nauseating smells, flies crawling over everything, filth, the cries of dying men, piteous. Believe me, you wouldn't want to know more details than that, and nothing I could say would make any of it understandable.'

'You must have been brave,' she said, 'to put up with it. To come through.'

'Brave? Nup. Scared witless. And as for putting up with it, well, no alternative really – simple as that. Take it from me, there's very little room in your head for brave thoughts when you're feeling so wretched.

'Anyhow, after my discharge, I was lucky enough to get cartage jobs around Wollongong for quite a few years, and then when the steelworks got going at Port Kembla they gave me a contract to bring regular supplies of coke from various collieries in the district. Good steady work it was, too, and I did all right for myself. Became fairly well known along the south coast. And that's how Aunt Muriel found out where I was. Word gets around. I suppose there weren't many Chinese blokes in New South Wales driving a carter's truck with the name George Lawson in big letters on the side of it.'

'When you call her Aunt Muriel,' said Harry, frowning at a stain on the tablecloth, 'it sounds as if she's *your* aunt, too.'

'She is. You and I are half-brothers.'

Harry leaned back in his chair. He clasped his hands on his head as if to hold this flighty idea in place so that he could think about it carefully. His mouth hung open but no words came out.

George took a cigarette from his packet and held it unlit. In his other hand he turned a matchbox over and over, looking down at it frequently as he spoke, as if it contained answers to all questions. The faint rattle of matches punctuated the rest of his story.

'After her sister died, you see,' he went on, 'Aunt Muriel felt able to make enquiries about me without upsetting anyone. She'd wanted to know my whereabouts but even the fact I existed had been a close secret for so long that she'd lost track of me when I went off to the war. She always thought the family should have kept me and looked after me. Our mother couldn't do it herself, an unmarried girl of seventeen. Her parents refused to let her hang on to me. They sent her off to a convent in Goulburn for her confinement, and insisted she give me to the nuns when I was born.'

Harry glimpsed the startled look on Nellie's face as this detail uncomfortably echoed part of her own story. George continued without seeming to notice her reaction.

'Then she went back to live with her parents, who made sure the Goulburn episode was hush-hush. So when your father came on the scene he was told nothing, and through all their married life he remained unaware of me. At least that's what Aunt Muriel presumes.'

He tossed the matchbox aimlessly onto the table, picking it up again at the same moment as he picked up his narrative.

'I wasn't aware of any of this myself until recently. Growing up, all I knew was that I had a name that didn't match my face, and that I'd been handed over to the Christian Brothers, and that someone was anonymously paying for my board and education. Well, it turns out that the "someone" was Aunt Muriel – and her husband. You see, Uncle Percy already had a good income and they'd wanted from the start to give me a home and have Lillian, my mother – our mother – live with them too; but our grandparents wouldn't allow it. There was a strict family rule of complete silence about me. So instead, Muriel and Percy quietly made sure I got a good education. Put up the money and arranged things with the school.'

Harry frowned. 'But where does your name come from? Lawson?'

'Well, I had no idea about that – didn't have a clue where I'd come from – until a couple of years ago, when Muriel caught up with me in Port Kembla. You can imagine it was a shock for me when this elderly woman came to my door and told me she was my aunt. Anyway, about the name: she said it's an anglicised form of my father's name. She and Percy persuaded my mother to have Lawson put on the birth certificate. He'd been employed, my father, on their parents' farm, you see, as a rouseabout, but he used to spend some of his time digging the vegetable garden behind the farmhouse, and that's how Lillian got talking with him. Muriel said it wasn't surprising her younger sister was sweet on him. He had a lovely gentle smile, she told me, and was very courteous, and quite tall for a Chinese man, being from Manchuria. His name was Law Sin or Loh Sin. When our grandfather found out whose baby it was, he went livid. Told Law Sin to leave the district at once or he'd come after him with a rifle.

'By the time Aunt Muriel came looking for me in Port Kembla, she was alone. Her husband Percy had passed away, and her sister too – our mother. Your father had died earlier. And of course our grandparents were long gone. I suppose it was because Muriel and Percy were childless that she was especially keen to find me before she got too frail for searching. Apart from you, and she'd lost contact with you, I was the only person left she could regard as a family member. Anyway, she made me promise to try to get in touch with you, and gave me a bit of money for the journey west, presuming you were still over here somewhere − and so here I am.'

Nellie broke the silence.

'You don't have any family of your own, George?'

'No. No wife, no kids, no-one. Not very marriageable, I'm afraid!' He laughed, but just with his mouth. 'Neither Chinese nor white, you see. A sort of in-between person. Nowhere for me to belong.'

'You're very welcome to stay with us for a while, George,' said Nellie.

After a week's conversations, Harry and George had relaxed into amicability. He was pleasant company. Harry could see that Nellie liked him too.

'I've been thinking about your name, George,' said Harry as they sat smoking after dinner one evening. 'Your surname, I mean. Funny thing is, a lot of people would say it's as Australian as you can get. Heard of Henry Lawson?'

George shook his head.

'He wrote ballads and stories about life in the bush. Mostly about how things seldom turn out the way people expect. My dad used to read some of Lawson's stories to me. Dry humour, sometimes sardonic, very Australian I suppose. Anyway, it just struck me that you share his name − but in both cases it was adopted in the process of turning an outsider into an Australian. Your Lawson comes from Law Sin, and his comes from Larsen. I remember Dad telling me that Henry Lawson's father was Norwegian. Similar handle to a fellow called Larrson who used to work with me. And oddly enough, one of my heroes has a name that sounds nearly the same – Mawson, the polar explorer, one of the most famous Australians, and he wasn't born in this country either! Mawson, Lawson, Law Sin, Larsen and Larrson – it all goes to show what a mongrel nation Australia really is, eh?'

~

'You two should go along on your own. It's not really my cup of tea. I can stay here, listen to the radio program.'

'No, George – we'd like you to come with us, wouldn't we, Harry? An event like this isn't just for couples. There'll be quite a few young women wanting dance partners, you can be sure of that. It's for a good cause, too.'

Harry nodded. 'And anyhow, with my wonky leg I'm not up to a full evening's exertion. If you come I can take a breather from time to time while you partner Nellie.'

Jaunty music bounced towards them as they approached the Town Hall. *Community dance here Saturday 8 p.m. to midnight*, said a large blackboard propped beside the street door. *Old time favourites and modern styles. All proceeds going to war effort.* They bought their tickets from an old crone at a table in the foyer. Coloured streamers bedecked the inside of the hall, and a large Union Jack was draped across the back of the stage, behind the musicians. A smaller Australian ensign was pinned to one of the side walls. The loudest sounds were coming from the accordionist who stood in front of the group, florid and rotund. A schottische finished just as Harry, Nellie and George entered the hall. The dancers applauded vigorously. Grinning, the accordionist grasped the microphone with both hands as if cheerfully throttling the life out of it. 'Thank you, ladies and gentlemen,' he barked. 'It's nice to be appreciated. I learned to play the accordion from my Uncle Pete – perhaps a few of you here remember him. Knew only one tune, "God Save the King", but he'd vary the tempo to suit the dance, so he could play waltz, polka, anything!' Everybody laughed.

'Now for the next dance, I'm going to take a rest, and so will our fiery fiddler Bert and our demon drummer Larry, because there's something special coming up this time. Yes, it's Bill Tucker with his amazing music saw! So take your partners please for the Destiny Waltz.'

A stooped old man with a fluffy beard like white fairy floss made his way to the front of the stage, leaned forward gingerly on an upright chair and squeezed the handle of a wood-cutting saw between his knees, with the serrated edge facing towards him. Holding its tip with his left hand, he began to move a violin bow across the outer side of the blade, which he bent slightly into an S-curve, twisting it a little this way or that to vary the sweet spot. And by jigging one of his bony legs while he played, he made the blade tremble so that it produced a ghostly vibrato. As the slow melody of the Destiny Waltz drew the couples dreamily around the dance floor, the elderly musician lifted his head for the first time and smiled a blessing at the circling crowd. Harry smiled too, feeling momentarily something near to serenity, and when the music stopped he clapped with as much enthusiasm as anyone there.

The saw-player shuffled off the platform and the regular group resumed their places for the next bracket, starting with a fast foxtrot. Harry led Nellie out on the floor and did his best to keep up with the quick-stepping rhythm, but his knee made him move stiffly and the dance seemed endless. When at last the music stopped he apologised for his lack of balance.

They walked back to where George stood watching them.

'Not very graceful on my part,' Harry said contritely. 'I'm in worse shape than I thought. George, can you take over from me for the next one or two?'

It was more than one or two. Harry sat or leaned against the wall for the rest of the evening, except when he went outside now and then for a cigarette. George and Nellie made a good pair, he thought, as they twirled their way smoothly through the Gay Gordons and the Gypsy Tap and the Veleta Waltz. They were laughing a lot, and talking animatedly. Rejoining him briefly between dances, they seemed to assume that he would remain on the sideline while they danced together for the rest of the evening. He didn't demur. Ah, let them enjoy themselves, he thought.

Over supper, when he had just put most of a jam-filled scone in his mouth, he turned away from the trestle table and bumped clumsily into someone.

'Elva!' he exclaimed, crumbs spilling from his lips. He wiped his mouth quickly with the back of his hand and corrected himself: 'Nurse Watkins. Or should I say Miss Watkins when you're not in uniform? Anyhow, it's good to see you. I hadn't spotted you in the crowd.'

'We arrived late. Just in time for the supper dance.'

'We?'

'I came with my fiancé, Joe McSkimming. That's him over there, talking to one of his mates. He's the dark-haired one.' She gestured towards two men in soldiers' uniform. 'They're based at the training camp. Joe's a farmer – his family has property near Beverley – but he's enlisted now.'

'Congratulations on the engagement.'

'Thank you.'

Harry thought she looked nearly as shy and uncomfortable as he felt himself. He wanted to say something that would restore the connection they used to have.

'Elva, I...' he began softly.

She interrupted hastily, 'Matron not here? Your wife?'

'Oh yes, she's just popped outside for a smoke, with a... friend of ours – someone from Sydney who's staying with us.'

'Well, I must be getting back to Joe.'

'Of course. Good luck to you both.'

He felt a twinge of sadness as she turned away. During those early weeks in the hospital bed he'd been able to talk with Elva so much more freely than he could nowadays with Nellie. The young nurse's calm, pleasant way of attending to his needs had quickly brought ease and candour into their conversations. In response to Elva, his words had begun to flow after years of increasing taciturnity. It was as if he had become, for a short while, almost youthful again. When she was at his bedside he'd felt enlivened, enthusiastic. He'd spoken lyrically about the particulars of the Grass Valley landscape – the way fields of oats in ear swayed and rustled in the wind, the satisfying labour of piling sheaves into golden stooks, the tawny colour that sunlight gave to the dust billowing behind a truck, or the jumble of spindly jam-trees on the rim of the hill that sloped up from the stables. He'd talked about the farm animals, too. He remembered her laughing delightedly at his description of a leggy foal's first tremulous steps as 'wobblesome'. And they'd chuckled together as he tried to imitate the sound of a crow relentlessly smacking a filched chunk of bony meat against the shed's iron roof and the answering yelps of indignant protest from the cattle dog, a coarse duet that had gone on for what seemed like hours.

With Nellie, lately, there had been hardly any conversations of that kind. His fluency had dwindled again.

He tried now to push those things out of his mind and bring his attention back to what was going on around him. The little band struck up again for more dancing. Harry recognised the song they were playing: 'Farewell to Dreams'. He had heard it often on the radio, sung by that mellifluous duo Nelson Eddy and Jeanette MacDonald. He hummed it to himself, recalling the words as the accordionist belted out the tune.

Must we say farewell to dreams,
To our hopes and our golden schemes?

He looked from Elva and her soldier fiancé to Nellie and George, and back to Elva again. The evening felt long. His life felt short.

George's stay in their house stretched to a fortnight, three weeks, a month. Harry found him likeable, and it was obvious that in Nellie's eyes George was more than likeable. To whatever he said she responded animatedly, sometimes flirtatiously.

I can recognise what's happening, Harry told himself. But he didn't have the heart to try to stop it. Although there were little spasms of jealousy and hurt pride, and two or three times he felt his fist tightening in his pocket, he tried to look at the situation rationally. It was obvious enough that his injuries – and perhaps some inherent weakness, too – had defaced his manliness, turning him into a shadow of what he once was, or imagined he'd be. George, in contrast, was personable, with all the self-confidence that comes from conquering difficulties. With the three of them under one roof, trouble was inevitable.

It was no surprise to see through the window, when he returned from the corner store one afternoon, that Nellie had come home early and that she and George were embracing in the kitchen. Her arms were around his neck. He had one hand inside her blouse while the other rubbed the top of her thigh. They sprang apart when Harry opened the back door. He made no fuss, just nodded to them, went on through to the front room, and lit a cigarette while he read the paper.

That evening at bedtime Harry told Nellie he would move out as soon as he could arrange somewhere to go.

'No hard feelings, Nellie,' he said resignedly. 'I'm not the man for you, I know that now. Perhaps George is. Good luck to you both anyhow.' He'd been rehearsing this simple speech in his mind for a couple of hours, discarding the impulse to reproach her.

She bit her lip, nodded, shed tears, and struggled to get out the word 'Sorry'.

He wrote to the Rivens, not saying much but explaining that he couldn't work because of injuries from an accident and asking whether they could put him up again for a while. Ruth sent a letter back promptly. They would be happy to see him. They didn't have a spare bedroom now that Rachel was too big to be put into a cot in her parents' room, but he'd be welcome to doss down in the little shed out the back.

A couple of weeks later he was on the train to Perth.

Nineteen

They sat around the pockmarked kitchen table, Ruth shelling peas into a chipped enamel basin while Patrick dandled young Rachel on his knee and Harry leaned back listening, arms folded.

'Perhaps there's something about being an only child,' Patrick was saying, 'that draws you intuitively towards another person with the same kind of family background. I sensed an affinity with Ruth straight away, and it may have had to do with the fact that neither of us has any siblings.'

'I'm an only child too,' Harry told them, forgetting momentarily about George. So is the person who is probably Ruth's mother, he thought, but he couldn't divulge what he believed he knew about the affinity. 'And yes,' he added, 'it probably does affect the way we relate to other people.'

'Rachel's looking sleepy,' said Ruth. 'Time to put her to bed.' Her daughter, with a tired smile, waved to the men as she was carried from the room.

Patrick turned to Harry. 'I've made a decision,' he said. 'I'm going to enlist. I told Ruth this morning. She doesn't want me to go, of course. And the prospect of being parted from the two of them – it's upsetting just to think about a long separation, let alone the possibility of never... You know. Gives me a sick feeling in my guts. But I can't hide behind others. If Australian men don't pull together and help to stop what Hitler's doing in Europe, it could roll around the world like a...like a huge surge of evil.' Patrick flung up his hand in a gesture that seemed both anxious and resolute.

'I can't quarrel with that,' said Harry. 'If I wasn't such an old crock,' he added regretfully, 'I'd be volunteering to serve overseas myself.'

'But for me it's a comfort to know you'll be staying here,' said Patrick, 'and can keep an eye on the home front for me.' The unspoken implication was clear: *in case I don't come back.*

'I'll look after them all right, don't fret about that. And there'll probably be something useful I can do here in Perth for the war effort, too. Perhaps to do with wireless, like last time, though I'm a bit rusty on the technical stuff nowadays.'

They remained for a while in sombre but companionable silence, grateful for the slight breeze that was now coming through the kitchen window. With Christmas less than three weeks away, the long swelter of a Perth summer was already taking early hold.

Sighing, Patrick inspected the palms of his hands as if his future could be read there. 'Day after next, I'll be in Northam with other army recruits. Intensive training before they ship us overseas.'

Harry nodded. He could see the strain of apprehension creasing the young man's forehead. His own thoughts wended back to the onset of the previous war. It was strange to picture himself as even younger, then, than Patrick was now. But at the time the whole world seemed to have a youthful outlook, with energy to burn. That earlier conflict had caught them all by surprise, preoccupied as they were until then with innocent projects of nation-building, like the grand scheme of a coastal ring of wireless stations. In those buoyant days before the first big war, when their newly federated country seemed so full of promise, he used to feel himself lifted along by a current of progress that would continue to carry him – and everyone – into a brighter future. Were they simply naive? Had it all been a foolish and cruel delusion?

Certainly the mood was very different now. Harry could see it in weary faces, hear it in worried conversations. Not a lot of smiles around, and most of the joking was mordant, sardonic. Wireless these days had little else to talk about but the war. People everywhere tuned in anxiously to all the evening news broadcasts, not wanting to miss anything. Patrick had set their mantel clock five minutes fast so that its loud striking of the hour would summon them to cluster around the radio in time to hear the newsreader's voice without distraction. They had to listen intently. The official cadences might try to reassure the populace but a faint undertone of menace was often audible, like a distant rumbling from sultry clouds.

Even before the war broke out, its long approaching shadow had seemed to draw gloomy stories into the field of public attention. Stories of dwindled hopes, crushed ideals. Not long ago the newspaper had carried an article about Arthur Richardson, the man whose 'remarkable ride' around Australia on his bicycle had once made him such a popular hero. Harry remembered Freddie Dingle telling the wireless station workers about Richardson's exploits. But this recent report was not only a retelling of that tale of past triumph; it also revealed a dark sequel. At his home in England, Richardson had recently died of a self-inflicted gunshot wound, after shooting his wife. The injuries sustained during the Great War had left him seriously disturbed, said the article.

Now, as Harry sat with Patrick in silence, a group of solitary phantoms shuffled through his memory in a slow procession. Behind the lonely figure of Richardson, that mad dog of a cyclist, came another one-time hero who'd ended his own life violently: Throssell the broken warrior. Then Sid Jeffryes, falling apart in the snowy southern wilderness as his head filled with static; and Freddie, too, gregarious on the surface but isolated by guilt and desperation.

The next week brought a cool change, but the rain held off. Harry had been waiting for the hot spell to break. He set out soon after breakfast, limped up to Canning Road and then westwards along it and over the bridge.

'Any special reason for revisiting Wireless Hill?' Ruth had asked when he told her where he'd decided to go that morning. There was something in the way she tilted her head that reminded Harry poignantly of Nellie as a young woman. It had crossed his mind that Ruth might perhaps be thinking of Freddie Dingle, and worrying about Harry's own mood.

'Not quite sure,' he'd said. 'Just feel drawn towards it, somehow. I've been remembering how we felt about it in those early days. Proud, I suppose that's the simplest way to put it. After all, we were constructing something we were sure would be important. Facing out towards a new era, so to speak.'

As he walked, his words echoed in his head. Pride wasn't always a bad thing. Perhaps his impulse to return there now, after a long while away, came also from nostalgia. Probably from mere curiosity as well. But he was half-hoping, too, without letting this become a fully formed idea, that he could sound out someone there at the station about an opportunity to…well, to contribute his knowledge in some way to coastal surveillance work or whatever might be needed. He could do with a decent wage, too. What he was getting from the odd jobs down at the zoo hardly sufficed to cover his board.

On the foreshore near the end of the bridge, a large cormorant − or a shag or a darter? he couldn't spot the difference − was holding open its dark wings, stretching them wide to dry its feathers. There seemed to be something unnervingly familiar about this gothic posture, and it came to him suddenly: Freddie Dingle, arms lifted out to either side as he flung himself upon a high crucifix of thin air. Harry shuddered, tried to shake the image out of his head, and turned his gaze to the assortment of buildings on the Applecross side of the bridge.

When he had first come this way, years before, the area was nearly empty of occupants. Now it looked lived in. Houses had taken shape along the streets, and he could see cars parked outside some of them, a bent old man crouched on a trestle while painting a shed wall, a pair of mothers walking with young children in tow. He stopped for a couple of minutes to admire the modern lines of the Applecross District Hall with its sturdy rotunda in front and squat tower behind, the structure of serried shoulder blocks making it into a kind of a compressed ziggurat, a monument to solid civic values. He knew it was a popular place for dances, picture shows and miscellaneous local events. Facing the Bridge Hotel, it seemed to be trying to outstare the pub drinkers on behalf of respectable habits of family recreation.

The road surface was a lot better than it used to be, and he made good progress, along to the point near the landmark fig tree, spreading its large leaden grey limbs where a side street diverged to loop up past the station workers' housing towards the hillcrest and the towering mast. A corpulent man wearing a carpenter's apron and tool-belt emerged from one of the cottages as Harry was walking past. They exchanged greetings.

'So what's going on here?' Harry asked.

'Just finishing off extensions to this place, Principal Fitter's Quarters. Then we're done. It's the last of the improvements. Brought in electric power, water heaters and all that to the staff housing. Septic tanks too. Families expect houses to provide a lot more than they used to.'

'Things busy up on the hilltop, I suppose?'

'That's right,' said the tubby one, a hand resting on his belly as if to soothe it while the other hand rummaged in a box beside a pile of planks. 'Where's that bloody tri-square got to?' he muttered. 'Busy's the word, yeh. Now that we're at war again, the Navy's going to use these houses, y'see. They've already taken control of the whole operation up the hill there, along with all the other stations around the coast.'

Harry went on up the steep curving track towards the crest, noting with surprise how extensively the vegetation had returned. The hillside that was stripped and scorched when he first saw it, and still had large bare sandy patches when he had come here half a dozen years ago, was now covered with scrub – blackboys, ground-hugging creepers, tufty grasses, fat-candled banksia bushes, skinny gum trees, things he didn't recognise. And perched on branches or flitting among the leaves or sheltering in shady recesses, a farrago of birds astonished him with their enviable exultancy. At the time of his arrival from Sydney twenty-seven years back, there was hardly a living non-human thing to be seen on the hill. Now small honeyeaters were tickling flowers flirtatiously while their wattlebird cousins squawked a strident protest at Harry's intrusion and unidentifiable twitterers shuttled through the foliage. In a bright green blur a brace of parrots slipped past on some obscurely urgent mission. Magpie choristers were rehearsing a gargled rondeau.

The cluster of buildings and the big machines inside them still looked much the same as when Harry had helped to set them up, but the officer in charge didn't hesitate to make it plain that there was no place for him on the staff of the wireless station.

'Thanks for your interest, Mr Hopewell,' he said, squaring his epauletted shoulders and running a fingertip over his Clark Gable moustache as he stood up to bring their brief conversation to a close. 'But we have plenty of able-bodied men to maintain essential services here.'

You didn't need to emphasise 'able-bodied', thought Harry resentfully, as he was ushered to the door. I saw your expression, you supercilious bugger, when I limped into the room and then couldn't give you a proper manly handshake.

⌒

Leg beginning to ache, hat tilted sideways to shield the left side of his face from sun-scorch, he made his way slowly back towards Como. He tried to remember some of the tunes that used to provide a rhythmic accompaniment in the days when he first walked around these parts. But today he didn't feel in a whistling mood. Back then, when there was spring in his step and ambition in his heart, it was inconceivable that at the age of forty-six he'd be down and out, single and lonely. No regular work, no decent prospects, no intimate companion, no place to call his own.

He thought of the letter he'd received a couple of days before from Nellie. She was going to move to New South Wales, she said, with George. She hoped Harry wouldn't make a fuss – would understand that it was time for her to 'make a fresh start'. There was surely no need for them to go through the difficult business of a divorce if he didn't mind just keeping quiet about their brief marital history. She intended to live with George as his wife. No-one over there would know she was already married.

Swallowing his bitterness, Harry had replied with a short note of reassurance: she could rely on him, he said, never to mention it. He was sorry he hadn't been a more satisfactory husband, and he wished her and George the very best of luck.

No point in saying more. No good reason to upbraid her. It was hardly Nellie's fault that he'd let an idealised image of her blight so much of his life. She'd had more than her own share of misfortune in the past. Let her be happy now, if she could.

Sweat ran down his neck. The home to which he was returning was not truly his, though it did provide him, thanks to the kindness of Patrick and Ruth, with a vicarious sense of the homely. These days – observing how Ruth interacted with young Rachel, helping them as best he could, picturing other households he had known, and recalling scenes from his own childhood – he often found himself pondering the nature of familial bonds. Blood was no guarantee of close relationships, nor even a necessary condition for being 'members of one another' – that strangely compelling phrase surfaced from somewhere; he couldn't recall the source. So what really constituted a family, and made it function as it should? He mulled over the question as he walked, wiping his forehead with a damp handkerchief.

In part, it seemed to him, families were shaped by the stories they shared. As children grew up, these stories could look back to cherished experiences, episodes that drew a family's members time and again through a process of recollecting and reinterpreting their inter-linkages. Or they could look forward, with tales of anticipation and aspiration that envisaged things to come and projected a future together.

But as Harry knew to his regret, the weft of narrative wasn't always available. Sometimes family members could not join the threads of their past into a common fabric whose pattern made sense to each of them. And sometimes there was nothing discernible on any future's horizon that each of them could yearn to reach. Yet for these families, bereft of cohesive, story-shaped understandings of their identity, some measure of meaning and solace might still be found in the simple animal warmth that linked kith and kin: in the comforting conjunction of bodies, wrapped around one another with the closeness of parents and litter-mate progeny and sometimes adopted waifs and hangers-on too, cuddling together in their den, sty, lair or burrow – or even in the nooks and nests of a zoo.

That train of thought led him to his little mate Hinkler, and brought a smile to his face as he walked. Back in the house he shared with the Rivens, he had a dependent of his own to look after.

Harry was now the adoptive protector of a scrawny young cat, rescued a month ago from the gutter in an unseasonable rainstorm. It had swiftly become, he acknowledged to himself, his surrogate child. In some ways it – in fact *he*, very definitely male – behaved more like a puppy than a kitten, sniffing at everything and following Harry all around the place, adhesive as a shadow. But his feline nature became instantly dominant whenever he went near the backyard pepper tree: he liked to sprint up its trunk and lurk in the foliage, apparently in the hope that some incautious bird would flutter within reach. Perhaps he imagined he could fly, if need be – or at least glide nimbly from branch to branch. But his reach exceeded his grasp. So Harry called him Hinkler.

Hinkler fully inhabited the moment. He doesn't aspire to anything that's different from the here and now, thought Harry, watching his small comrade curl into himself, all presence. He doesn't worry about what lies ahead for civilisation. He takes no thought for the morrow. He toils not, neither does he spin.

Hinkler was by no means a productive member of the household. If he had been less indolent he might have earned his keep as a mouser. If he had been less timid he might have posed as a guardian of the premises. 'But you're no watch-cat, are you?' Harry liked to say to him with a regretful shake of his head. Hinkler would yawn, give a shrug of nonchalant concurrence, and return to his primary pastime of licking himself. He had no useful function whatsoever – except that, being (despite his air of aloofness) such a shamelessly dependent creature, he assigned all caretaking duties to

Harry, who thereby acquired a useful function himself. The knowledge that Hinkler relied on him for food, shelter and affectionate pampering gave Harry a quasi-parental sense of responsibility. This, he supposed, was something close to being part of a family.

Hinkler communicated with his guardian through a range of noises, from squeaking to yawping. And then there was all the purring, remarkably varied in its modulations. Sometimes it could seem as loud as an idling tractor motor. At other times his purr would subside into a whispered warble, like a pigeon with a sore throat.

~

In his little backyard room in Como, with Hinkler on his lap, Harry slowly turned the pages of the day's newspaper. War bulletins and reports from European correspondents dominated the international pages. Headlines blared at him:

EYES ON GENEVA — NAZIS WATCH NEUTRALS

AIR TRAINING — AUSTRALIA'S INTENTIONS

WESTERN FRONT ACTIVITY — PATROLS AND GUNFIRE

He felt impotent. With thousands of young Australian men already on their way into that arena of turmoil, and Patrick soon to be caught up in some part of it too, he himself could do little but watch from a distance, and try to give practical support to Patrick's family.

Harry let his thoughts drift. Nellie and George came into his mind; probably he'd never hear from them again. And Elva: he pictured her, moving briskly around the ward, pulling the partition around his bed, leaning over him, washing and drying him — and he felt bereft of what had briefly seemed an incipient friendship. The startled look on her face when she saw how he and Nellie recognised each other would always stay with him. He half-wished he could see Elva again, but knew it was a foolish impulse. Especially now that she was engaged and he had a duty to keep an eye on Ruth and the infant.

Not to mention Hinkler.

That night Harry was woken, as so often now, by an insistent paw tapping him on the shoulder and a gentle sound that was almost a soft kind of snoring. As he opened a bleary eye he saw Hinkler's face an inch from his own. A long feline whisker, antenna-like, tickled Harry's nostril. He sighed, lifted the sheet with his knees to make a kitten-sized tent, and curled a fatherly arm around the scraggy little beast. Under the covers, Hinkler snuggled against his belly, nestling and purring and trusting.

It's not the life I'd imagined, thought Harry sleepily. This isn't the Australia I thought I'd be living in. What came over the horizon in my direction wasn't lucky, and some things haven't turned out well for me. But I don't need to fold inwards on myself and give up the ghost. I'd like to reach out to people. Elva said I have a flair for storytelling, and there are plenty of tales to tell. If I write well about things I've seen and done, felt, desired, lost and found, it can be consonant with the experience of others because much of it, the good and the bad, touches on what has happened in the wider world. I'll put my mind to it.

Meanwhile I'm hardly alone. In a bedroom just a few yards away there's a young woman who's quite probably my step-daughter, though I'll never be able to let her know that I've been briefly married to the person I believe is her mother.

And there's her infant daughter, just beginning to walk and put sounds together – Rachel's almost like my secret granddaughter. I can talk with the pair of them every day, and do simple domestic things for them around the house, and look after them, and feel as if I belong. And here are Hinkler and I in our little hut nearby, rubbing along together companionably. It's not an empty existence. I think I can find in it something that approaches contentment.

Unblinking, he looked deep into the darkness and began to whistle softly.

Afterword

Living near Wireless Hill Park for many years, walking often around the bush-clad site and occasionally looking through the buildings that now comprise the Telecommunications Museum there, I formed the idea of writing a novel that would (among other things) reflect the role of this place in the history of Australian radio.

In 1912 the Commonwealth Government ambitiously utilised the newest technology of the day to construct a wireless station on a hill that was then part of the southern Perth suburb of Applecross, looking out over a broad expanse of the Swan River. The station remained in continuous use for more than half a century as the main coastal radio communications centre for Western Australia, and also played a part in the establishment of commercial broadcasting in this state. In 1969, after the Overseas Telecommunications Commission ceased operations at the station, the site was vested in the City of Melville. It was subsequently classified by the National Trust and listed on the National Estate Register.

I looked through a fascinating assortment of documents, photographs, and other historical materials relating to the Wireless Hill station that are held in the Melville Local Studies

Collection, as well as many items within the museum precinct (the former station itself), and I gladly acknowledge here the research assistance generously provided by Kaylene Poon and Soula Veyradier, respectively the Local History Officer and Curator/ Cultural Development Officer with the City of Melville. Of particular archival interest was a typescript of reminiscences by J. M. Johnson, who came from Sydney to Perth to work as a junior engineer on the building and equipping of the Applecross station. But I should emphasise that, apart from the very broad similarity of situation, my Harry Hopewell does not resemble Mr Johnson. A few details from the latter's memoir suggested indirectly some incidents and ideas from which parts of the story developed, but Harry, like every other character who appears in the foreground of the novel, is wholly imaginary; I have invented all his experiences and relationships.

I found other useful information about the early days of Wireless Hill in the Battye Library, especially in a typescript by Michael Cullity, *A History of Wireless Hill Melville: 1912–1967* and in the files of the Heritage Council of Western Australia. I also read a number of accounts of the early days of radio, notably Gavin Weightman, *Signor Marconi's Magic Box* (London, Harper Collins, 2003); Lesley Johnson, *The Unseen Voice: A Cultural Study of Early Australian Radio* (Routledge, London, 1988); R. R. Walker, *The Magic Spark: The Story of the First Fifty Years of Radio in Australia* (Melbourne, Hawthorn Press, 1973); and a chapter by Bridget Griffen-Foley, 'Modernity, Intimacy and Early Australian Commercial Radio,' in Joy Damousi and Desley Deacon (eds), *Talking and Listening in the Age of Modernity: Essays on the History of Sound* (Canberra, ANU EPress, 2007).

The development of radio is only one of the threads in my novel. For insights into various aspects of the social history of Perth and other Western Australian locations in the early twentieth century, I am especially indebted to the following sources: Geoffrey Bolton, *A Fine Country to Starve In* (UWA Press, 1972); W. S. Cooper and G. McDonald, *A City for All Seasons: The Story of Melville* (City of Melville, 1989); Phillip Pendal and Kerry Davey (eds), *South Perth: The Vanishing Village* (City of South Perth Historical Society, 2002); F. K. Crowley, *A History of South Perth* (Adelaide, Rigby, 1962); *Cecil Florey, Peninsular City: A Social History of the City of South Perth* (City of South Perth, 1995); Donald S. Garden, *Northam: An Avon Valley History* (Melbourne, Oxford University Press, 1979); Jan Ryan, *Ancestors: Chinese in Colonial Australia* (Fremantle Arts Centre Press, 1995); Paul Jones, *Chinese–Australian Journeys: Records on Travel, Migration and Settlement, 1860–1975* (Research Guide no. 21, National Archives of Australia, Canberra, 2005); Gerhard Fischer, *Enemy Aliens: Internment and the Homefront Experience in Australia, 1914–1920* (St. Lucia, University of Queensland Press, 1989); Victoria Hobbs, *But Westward Look: Nursing in Western Australia 1829–1979* (UWA Press, 1980); Harry Gordon (ed.), *An Eyewitness History of Australia* (Melbourne, Currey O'Neil, rev edn 1981); Arthur Richardson, *The Story of a Remarkable Ride* (Dunlop Pneumatic Tyre Co., 1900); W. K. Beckingham, *Red Acres: Thirty Years in the North-eastern Wheatbelt of Western Australia* (n.p., 1979). I also took snippets of detail from numerous pamphlets, photographs, website documents, and other miscellaneous materials too various to remember, let alone itemise.

Useful historical information about Perth Zoo, with a selection of photographs, is conveniently accessible in the archives held at Heritage House Cultural Centre in South Perth, and I wish to record the valuable practical assistance I received from the late Lavone Varendorf, former coordinator of the Local Studies Collection there. I also drew on some items from the zoo's own excellent website, and on a lyrical description of the zoo in its early years provided by May Vivienne, *Travels in Western Australia* (London, William Heinemann, 1902).

To check points about some historical figures hovering in the background of my novel, such as Douglas Mawson, Arthur Richardson and George Taylor, I consulted that rich online resource *The Australian Dictionary of Biography*. For details of Arctic and Antarctic exploration, I went directly to Sir Douglas Mawson, *The Home of the Blizzard: Being the Story of the Australasian Antarctic Expedition, 1911–1914* (1915; reprinted Adelaide, Wakefield Press, 2009), and also found material of incidental interest in Jeff Maynard, *Wings of Ice* (Sydney, Random House, 2010).

I am deeply grateful to a number of friends: in particular to Geoffrey Bolton, Paul Genoni and Andrew Taylor, who cheerfully agreed to read the novel in draft form and provided encouraging comments and constructive suggestions; to Brenda Walker, Paul Rossiter and Philip Gardiner, who helped with various kinds of timely practical information and advice; to those whose appreciative remarks about my previous novel gave me confidence in the writing of this one; to my vigilant and discerning editor Linda Martin and the whole exemplary team at UWAP, led with admirable verve by Terri-ann White; and to Gale MacLachlan, my most indispensable literary interlocutor and enduring companion.